Clover's Parent Fix

Clover's Parent Fix

Shana Muldoon Zappa and Ahmet Zappa
with Zelda Rose

Disney Press

Los Angeles • New York

Copyright © 2016 Disney Enterprises, Inc.

All rights reserved. Published by Disney Press, an imprint of Disney
Book Group. No part of this book may be reproduced or transmitted
in any form or by any means, electronic or mechanical, including
photocopying, recording, or by any information storage and retrieval
system, without written permission from the publisher.
For information address Disney Press,
1101 Flower Street, Glendale, California 91201.

Printed in the United States of America
Reinforced Binding
First Paperback Edition, July 2016
1 3 5 7 9 10 8 6 4 2

FAC-025438-16141

Library of Congress Control Number: 2016930865
ISBN 978-1-4847-1430-0

For more Disney Press fun, visit www.disneybooks.com

SUSTAINABLE FORESTRY INITIATIVE
Certified Chain of Custody
Promoting Sustainable Forestry
www.sfiprogram.org
SFI-01054
The SFI label applies to the text stock

Halo Violetta Zappa. You are pure light, joy, and inspiration. We love you soooooo much.

May the Star Darlings continue to shine brightly upon you. May every step upon your path be blessed with positivity and the understanding that you have the power within you to manifest the most fulfilling life you can possibly dream of and more. May you always remember that being different and true to yourself makes your inner star shine brighter. And never ever stop making wishes.

Glow for it. . . .
Mommy and Daddy

And to everyone else here on "Wishworld":

May you realize that no matter where you are in life, no matter what you look like or where you were born, you, too, have the power within you to create the life of your dreams. Through celebrating your own uniqueness, thinking positively, and taking action, you can make your wishes come true. May you understand that you are never alone. There is always someone near who will understand you if you look hard enough. The Star Darlings are here to remind you that there is an unstoppable energy to staying positive, wishing, and believing in yourself. That inner star shines within you.

Smile. The Star Darlings have your back. We know how startastic you truly are.

Glow for it. . . .
Your friends,
Shana and Ahmet

Student Reports

NAME: Clover
BRIGHT DAY: January 5
FAVORITE COLOR: Purple
INTERESTS: Music, painting, studying
WISH: To be the best songwriter and DJ on Starland
WHY CHOSEN: Clover has great self-discipline, patience, and willpower. She is creative, responsible, dependable, and extremely loyal.
WATCH OUT FOR: Clover can be hard to read and she is reserved with those she doesn't know. She's afraid to take risks and can be a wisecracker at times.
SCHOOL YEAR: Second
POWER CRYSTAL: Panthera
WISH PENDANT: Barrette

* • • * • • * • • * • • *

NAME: Adora
BRIGHT DAY: February 14
FAVORITE COLOR: Sky blue
INTERESTS: Science, thinking about the future and how she can make it better
WISH: To be the top fashion designer on Starland
WHY CHOSEN: Adora is clever and popular and cares about the world around her. She's a deep thinker.
WATCH OUT FOR: Adora can have her head in the clouds and be thinking about other things.
SCHOOL YEAR: Third
POWER CRYSTAL: Azurica
WISH PENDANT: Watch

NAME: Piper
BRIGHT DAY: March 4
FAVORITE COLOR: Seafoam green
INTERESTS: Composing poetry and writing in her dream journal
WISH: To become the best version of herself she can possibly be and to share that by writing books
WHY CHOSEN: Piper is giving, kind, and sensitive. She is very intuitive and aware.
WATCH OUT FOR: Piper can be dreamy, absentminded, and wishy-washy. She can also be moody and easily swayed by the opinions of others.
SCHOOL YEAR: Second
POWER CRYSTAL: Dreamalite
WISH PENDANT: Bracelets

Starling Academy

NAME: Astra
BRIGHT DAY: April 9
FAVORITE COLOR: Red
INTERESTS: Individual sports
WISH: To be the best athlete on Starland—to win!
WHY CHOSEN: Astra is energetic, brave, clever, and confident. She has boundless energy and is always direct and to the point.
WATCH OUT FOR: Astra is sometimes cocky, self-centered, condescending, and brash.
SCHOOL YEAR: Second
POWER CRYSTAL: Quarrelite
WISH PENDANT: Wristbands

NAME: Tessa
BRIGHT DAY: May 18
FAVORITE COLOR: Emerald green
INTERESTS: Food, flowers, love
WISH: To be successful enough that she can enjoy a life of luxury
WHY CHOSEN: Tessa is warm, charming, affectionate, trustworthy, and dependable. She has incredible drive and commitment.
WATCH OUT FOR: Tessa does not like to be rushed. She can be quite stubborn and often says no. She does not deal well with change and is prone to exaggeration. She can be easily sidetracked.
SCHOOL YEAR: Third
POWER CRYSTAL: Gossamer
WISH PENDANT: Brooch

NAME: Gemma
BRIGHT DAY: June 2
FAVORITE COLOR: Orange
INTERESTS: Sharing her thoughts about almost anything
WISH: To be valued for her opinions on everything
WHY CHOSEN: Gemma is friendly, easygoing, funny, extroverted, and social. She knows a little bit about everything.
WATCH OUT FOR: Gemma talks—a lot—and can be a little too honest sometimes and offend others. She can have a short attention span and can be superficial.
SCHOOL YEAR: First
POWER CRYSTAL: Scatterite
WISH PENDANT: Earrings

Student Reports

NAME: Cassie
BRIGHT DAY: July 6
FAVORITE COLOR: White
INTERESTS: Reading, crafting
WISH: To be more independent and confident and less fearful
WHY CHOSEN: Cassie is extremely imaginative and artistic. She is a voracious reader and is loyal, caring, and a good friend. She is very intuitive.
WATCH OUT FOR: Cassie can be distrustful, jealous, moody, and brooding.
SCHOOL YEAR: First
POWER CRYSTAL: Lunalite
WISH PENDANT: Glasses

NAME: Leona
BRIGHT DAY: August 16
FAVORITE COLOR: Gold
INTERESTS: Acting, performing, dressing up
WISH: To be the most famous pop star on Starland
WHY CHOSEN: Leona is confident, hardworking, generous, open-minded, optimistic, caring, and a strong leader.
WATCH OUT FOR: Leona can be vain, opinionated, selfish, bossy, dramatic, and stubborn and is prone to losing her temper.
SCHOOL YEAR: Third
POWER CRYSTAL: Glisten paw
WISH PENDANT: Cuff

NAME: Vega
BRIGHT DAY: September 1
FAVORITE COLOR: Blue
INTERESTS: Exercising, analyzing, cleaning, solving puzzles
WISH: To be the top student at Starling Academy
WHY CHOSEN: Vega is reliable, observant, organized, and very focused.
WATCH OUT FOR: Vega can be opinionated about everything, and she can be fussy, uptight, critical, arrogant, and easily embarrassed.
SCHOOL YEAR: Second
POWER CRYSTAL: Queezle
WISH PENDANT: Belt

Starling Academy

NAME: Libby
BRIGHT DAY: October 12
FAVORITE COLOR: Pink
INTERESTS: Helping others, interior design, art, dancing
WISH: To give everyone what they need—both on Starland and through wish granting on Wishworld
WHY CHOSEN: Libby is generous, articulate, gracious, diplomatic, and kind.
WATCH OUT FOR: Libby can be indecisive and may try too hard to please everyone.
SCHOOL YEAR: First
POWER CRYSTAL: Charmelite
WISH PENDANT: Necklace

* * • * • • • * • • * • • *

NAME: Scarlet
BRIGHT DAY: November 3
FAVORITE COLOR: Black
INTERESTS: Crystal climbing (and other extreme sports), magic, thrill seeking
WISH: To live on Wishworld
WHY CHOSEN: Scarlet is confident, intense, passionate, magnetic, curious, and very brave.
WATCH OUT FOR: Scarlet is a loner and can alienate others by being secretive, arrogant, stubborn, and jealous.
SCHOOL YEAR: Third
POWER CRYSTAL: Ravenstone
WISH PENDANT: Boots

* * • * • • • * • • * • • *

NAME: Sage
BRIGHT DAY: December 1
FAVORITE COLOR: Lavender
INTERESTS: Travel, adventure, telling stories, nature, and philosophy
WISH: To become the best Wish-Granter Starland has ever seen
WHY CHOSEN: Sage is honest, adventurous, curious, optimistic, friendly, and relaxed.
WATCH OUT FOR: Sage has a quick temper! She can also be restless, irresponsible, and too trusting of others' opinions. She may jump to conclusions.
SCHOOL YEAR: First
POWER CRYSTAL: Lavenderite
WISH PENDANT: Necklace

Introduction

You take a deep breath, about to blow out the candles on your birthday cake. Clutching a coin in your fist, you get ready to toss it into the dancing waters of a fountain. You stare at your little brother as you each hold an end of a dried wishbone, about to pull. But what do you do first?

You make a wish, of course!

Ever wonder what happens right after you make that wish? *Not much*, you may be thinking.

Well, you'd be wrong.

Because something quite unexpected happens next. Each and every wish that is made becomes a glowing Wish Orb, invisible to the human eye. This undetectable orb zips through the air and into the heavens, on a one-way trip to the brightest star in the sky—a magnificent place called Starland. Starland is inhabited by Starlings, who look a lot like you and me, except they have a sparkly glow to their skin, and glittery hair in unique colors. And they have one more thing: magical powers. The Starlings use these powers to make good wishes come true, for when good wishes are granted, the result is positive energy. And the Starlings of Starland need this energy to keep their world running.

In case you are wondering, there are three kinds of Wish Orbs:

1) GOOD WISH ORBS. These wishes are positive and helpful and come from the heart. They are pretty and sparkly and are nurtured in climate-controlled Wish-Houses. They bloom into fantastical glowing orbs. When the time is right, they are presented to the appropriate Starling for wish fulfillment.

2) BAD WISH ORBS. These are for selfish, mean-spirited, or negative things. They don't sparkle

at all. They are immediately transported to a special containment center, as they are very dangerous and must not be granted.

3) IMPOSSIBLE WISH ORBS. These wishes are for things, like world peace and disease cures, that simply can't be granted by Starlings. These sparkle with an almost impossibly bright light and are taken to a special area of the Wish-House with tinted windows to contain the glare they produce. The hope is that one day they can be turned into good wishes the Starlings can help grant.

Starlings take their wish granting very seriously. There is a special school called Starling Academy that accepts only the best and brightest young Starling girls. They study hard for four years, and when they graduate, they are ready to start traveling to Wishworld to help grant wishes. For as long as anyone can remember, only graduates of wish-granting schools have ever been allowed to travel to Wishworld. But things have changed in a very big way.

Read on for the rest of the story. . . .

Prologue

Together we face the music.
Together we take a stand.
We're one for all and all for one.
We're the members of the band.

Clover paused, Star-Zap in hand, as she swung slowly back and forth on her hammock, composing a song.

At least, Clover was *trying* to compose a song. She was the main songwriter for the Star Darlings band, although—by her own choice—she wasn't an official member. Clover could play just about any instrument on Starland—from the keytar to the googlehorn—and had a true stage presence. But she was taking a break from the starlight. After all those staryears performing with her circus family—traveling with "The Greatest Show on Starland"—she wanted to concentrate on her real love: songwriting.

If only this song was coming easier! It was supposedly about Star Darlings the band. But it was really about Star Darlings the star-charmed group of students fated to save their world. And Clover was having a tough time with it, despite her strategies.

First: to set a goal. And that was to finish the song before the Battle of the Bands competition.

Second: to keep to a routine. And she did, working first thing in the morning, before breakfast, even if inspiration didn't hit . . . even if she'd stayed up late the night before and wanted extra sleep. *Even now,* she thought.

Across the room, Clover heard her roommate, Astra, tossing a star ball into a net. *Thump, thump, thump.* It was the perfect backbeat.

She returned to work.

Together we face the music.
Together we sing our song.

We've faced a lot of startrouble,
But we always stay starstrong.

Strength. Clover considered how strong each Star Darling had to be. Every mission they'd gone on had been riddled with problems: mixed-up Wisher and wish identifications, for starters, and Leona's Wish Pendant's burning up on the trip back. And poor Adora, whose Wishworld transformation hadn't lasted one starday. Sparkly and glowing, she'd had to hide in a bathroom!

Of course there was Scarlet, too, whose trouble had started before her mission even began. She'd been kicked out of the Star Darlings and replaced by a girl named Ophelia. Lady Stella, the headmistress, had claimed Ophelia was the true Star Darling. Luckily, Scarlet wound up collecting wish energy anyway. But had Lady Stella switched the girls to mess up another mission? Clover hated to admit it, but it certainly seemed that way. In fact, all the evidence pointed to Lady Stella as the evil mastermind behind the problems. And that included both the poisonous flowers that had made the Star Darlings bicker and the toxic nail polish that had made them act so strange.

Did she have an accomplice? There was that mysterious woman Astra kept spotting having meetings with

Lady Stella. What did it all mean? And what could the Star Darlings do about it?

Clover wanted a faster beat to match all those questions. Something with an edge. Astra began to bounce two star balls at once. Double time.

Clover picked up the rhythm.

What is Starland's fate, fate, fate?
It's time to lend a hand, hand, hand.
We're all in sync, sync, sync.
We're the Star Darlings band, band, band.

Fate. That was a powerful refrain, Clover thought—for the song *and* for the Star Darlings themselves. Tessa, Cassie, and Scarlet had discovered a secret underground chamber holding an ancient prophecy, a book proclaiming that twelve Star-Charmed Starlings were destined to save Starland. (And it was clear now that Starland was certainly in trouble and needed saving! Power outages and energy blips had become frighteningly common.)

Of course the Star Darlings figured out they were those very Starlings—just before getting trapped inside the chamber. *Thank the stars we found them,* Clover thought. But was that another evil act by Lady Stella?

Clover slowed down the tempo.

Oh, we believe in the truth.
Please don't tell us these lies.
We believe in the stars
Shining high above in the skies.

Hmmm. Clover considered the next lines. The Star Darlings had confronted Lady Stella, demanding the truth. But what would Clover write about that meeting? How Lady Stella had—

Clover's Star-Zap flickered and chimed with a holo-call. She glanced at the screen. It was her mom, hanging upside down on a trapeze. In the background Clover saw the circus big top, the view swinging wildly as her mom moved back and forth.

These trapeze calls could last for starhours. Each time her mom swung past another relative, she'd pass the Star-Zap. Clover bit her lip. She was just getting started on these lyrics. But it meant so much to her family, particularly her mom, to talk to her. She swiped the screen and a holo-image appeared in the air before her.

"Hello, darling," said her mother, still swinging. "We just set up the tent in Old Prism for tonight's show."

"That's great, Mom," said Clover. "How is it going?"

"Well . . ." Her mom's trapeze slowed as she thought things over. "We're running behind, actually. Our circus swift train had to pull over and recharge a few times."

Just then Clover's dad grabbed the Star-Zap as he swung from the opposite direction. "Nothing to worry about, Clover!" He jumped off at the platform, passing the phone to her aunt Cecile.

Cecile held the device with one hand as she grabbed the trapeze with the other. She soared through the air, and Clover saw a dizzying stream of colors. "The show will definitely be late," her aunt said chattily. "And our clown car lost its shrink/expand energy, so it can't hold a hydrong clowns anymore."

Aunt Cecile let go of the trapeze, aiming for Clover's mom's outstretched arms.

"Now that clown car can barely hold your great-grandfather Otto!" her mom said, neatly catching Aunt Cecile and taking the Star-Zap at the same time.

So the wish energy shortage is really everywhere now, Clover thought. The high-energy circus, seemingly immune to negativity, was the last place she thought would be hit. "But are you doing okay?" she asked.

"We're right as starshine," her mom said, delivering her aunt to another swing. "Just some minor inconveniences. Let me show you my new dive into a barrel of water."

But Clover's Star-Zap buzzed with a holo-text. The barrel dive would have to wait. She had received an all-school message marked READ IMMEDIATELY.

PLEASE REPORT TO THE AUDITORIUM AS SOON AS STAR-POSSIBLE FOR AN IMPORTANT ANNOUNCEMENT, it read.

In Clover's two years at Starling Academy, there had never been a major meeting called unexpectedly.

Whatever it was, it had to be big.

CHAPTER
1

An important announcement! The whole school had to be there! Would the assembly be about Lady Stella and her role in the energy shortage? About her sabotage?

Clover flipped out of her hammock, landing perfectly on two feet with her arms high above her head. The somersault was really just a habit. But still she glanced at Astra to see if her roommate had noticed.

Astra, a star athlete, had recently returned from Wishworld, where she'd helped grant the wish of a young gymnast and had gone to a competition. Now Astra was projecting a holo-sign with the score 999,999.5.

"Starf!" said Clover. "Half a point more and I'd have a perfect moonium."

"Better luck next time," Astra said. "And I'm sure there will be a next time."

"And I'm sure you'll be there to judge me," Clover shot back with a grin.

Acrobatic tricks, kidding around—it all came naturally to Clover. Growing up as part of the Flying Molensa Family, Clover had been surrounded by generations of aunts, uncles, and cousins—not to mention her own parents and siblings—who could walk a tightrope while juggling a glowzen ozziefruits and cracking jokes. Living with Astra had always been a breeze. But living in a dorm at Starling Academy was another story.

Before school, Clover had never stayed anywhere for more than a starweek. She and her family traveled year-round across Starland, living out of suitcases on the circus swift train.

Clover had shared a sleeping car with her sisters and she'd always had an upper berth. That was why she loved her hammock bed. It reminded her of the gentle motion of the moving swift train.

"So," said Astra, slipping into her sneakers, "I wonder who will be making this big announcement. Surely not Lady Stella."

Wouldn't it be starmazing, though, if Lady Stella called

the assembly and everything is back to normal? Clover thought with a sigh. She imagined the school day proceeding just as it always had, with no energy blips, no upheaval, and Lady Stella just where she should be.

"Starland to Clover! Starland to Clover!" Astra snapped her fingers star inches from Clover's face. "Come on. We'd better hurry. If the entire school is going to the Astral Auditorium, it will be crowded."

Clover nodded. She picked up her hat and placed it on her head, making sure it curved just right. The purple fedora had been handed down to her by her great-grandma Sunny, and Clover planned to pass it down to her own grandchild one starday. It set off her sparkly eyes and short bouncy hair, matching their deep purple shade almost perfectly. She rarely went out without it.

"Ready," she told Astra.

The two Starlings headed outside and jumped onto the already crowded Cosmic Transporter. All around them, girls chatted excitedly, making guesses about the important announcement.

"Hey, Clover!" a third-year student named Aurora called out. "Maybe Lady Stella is canceling classes because your family is performing."

Last staryear, Clover's family had visited, and Lady

Stella had announced a holiday so the students could watch their show. Everyone had agreed the best part was when Professor Dolores Raye had been invited into the star-ring.

Professor Dolores Raye was short—in size and temperament—and wore serious large-framed glasses. She was no one's favorite teacher. So when Clover's dad had offered her his arm and led her to a cosmic cannon, the students watched with interest. Clearly the humorless teacher hadn't wanted to become a Starling cannonball. But at that point, there was no turning back. Clover's dad lit the fuse with a wish energy snap of his fingers, and she'd flown through the air.

"There's no landing pad!" Lady Cordial had screeched in panic.

Everyone gasped. But Clover's dad slowed the flight with a wave of his arm, and Professor Dolores Raye landed safely on her feet.

It had been fun. But today's announcement had nothing to do with her family, Clover felt sure.

"No, no," she quickly said. "The circus isn't coming!"

"Well, maybe Lady Stella will hand out the Triple S award today," someone else guessed.

The Silver Shining Star was the highest honor in all of Starling Academy, given to a student who had received starperlative assessments in the classroom, in the school community, and in her hometown.

"Maybe," Clover said pleasantly. She'd be starprised if this announcement brought any good news. But she couldn't share her thoughts with anyone but a Star Darling.

Once they were outside, three other Star Darlings walked up behind Clover and Astra: first year Libby and sisters Tessa and Gemma. They all looked worried.

"Star greetings," Gemma said in a quiet voice—at least, quiet for Gemma. As the Cosmic Transporter moved along, she kept up a steady stream of chatter, touching on everything but Lady Stella and the announcement. She could hardly be blamed, Clover thought, only half listening. They couldn't discuss anything there, in public. Only sweet-tempered, pink-haired Libby paid attention to Gemma, nodding at every statement.

"Did you hear that noise?" Gemma said in a much louder voice. "That rumbling sound? Something must be wrong with the transporter! Remember when it ran out of power just the other—"

"Relax, Gemma," Tessa said irritably. "It's only my stomach. You do know breakfast is postponed because of this assembly, don't you? It's really not fair. Some of us need to eat on a regular schedule."

Clover understood the part about keeping a schedule. She liked to have a predictable timetable, too. But how could Tessa be concerned about food at a time like this? "Tessa—" she began to scold.

But then Piper slid into place beside her and put a reassuring hand on her arm. How did Piper do that, always appear seemingly out of thin air? "Relax, Clover," she said in a soothing voice. "Tessa isn't really worried about breakfast. It's just transtarence—'transference,' as Wishlings would say."

"Transtarence?" Clover repeated. Sometimes Piper had an intuitive sense of others' thoughts and feelings, but sometimes she was way off starbase. Which was it now?

"Yes. Tessa is transferring, or redirecting, her concern about Lady Stella—to food!" Piper finished in a whisper.

Ahead, the Cosmic Transporter was emptying, and Clover realized they had reached the auditorium. She linked arms with Astra and Piper and—with Gemma, Tessa, and Libby close behind—followed the crowd.

Just outside the auditorium doors, the rest of the Star Darlings waited.

"Over here!" Leona waved her arms dramatically, her golden curls bouncing. Cassie stood next to her, looking pale. She seemed to be holding on to the arm of her roommate, Sage, for support. The two had disagreed about Lady Stella—Sage supporting the headmistress, Cassie opposing her. Sage had a strong personality. But shy, quiet Cassie had stood her ground, convincing the Star Darlings that Lady Stella was the enemy.

Now, looking at Cassie's conflicted expression, Clover wondered if she might be having second thoughts. Scarlet, a short distance away from the others, looked defiantly at anyone who so much as glanced in her direction.

Meanwhile, Adora and Vega, their blue heads of hair almost blending into one, were huddled over one of Vega's puzzle holo-books. "Hey! Aren't there any science questions?" Adora complained. More transtarence, Clover decided.

"Come on!" Sage said impatiently. "Let's go inside."

The Star Darlings stepped into the auditorium. At the very same starmin, a student named Vivica—just about the meanest girl in school, Clover thought—elbowed her way past, her own group of friends trailing her.

Vivica stopped abruptly and the girl directly behind her tripped, crashing into Clover.

"Star apologies!" the girl told Vivica, ignoring Clover. "I should have been paying more attention."

Vivica sniffed. "Be more careful next time, Brenna." Then she turned to Clover. "As for you, I suggest you try harder to keep up with the crowd. Those SDs," she muttered to her friends. "They really are superbly dense!"

Clover ignored her. The Cycle of Life was too short to let Vivica get on her nerves. Unfortunately, she wound up sitting directly behind her in the auditorium.

"I'm really wondering about this big announcement," Vivica was saying to Brenna.

"If it is the Triple S award," Brenna said, "you'll be a star-in."

"Me? Getting the Triple S?" said Vivica with loud false modesty. "Why would they ever give it to little old me? Yes, I was the champion light-skater at the Luminous Lake competition. And I earn all Is in my classes. Illumination, Illumination, Illumination. That's all my star report says! And of course, there's the band I put together. We're totally stellar. Still . . . the award?"

The lights brightened, signaling the students to be quiet. Then Lady Cordial shuffled to center stage. She gazed around nervously, gripping a microphone in one hand. She tucked a loose strand of purple hair behind her ear, and the mic hit her head. A loud screech sounded, reaching the last rows.

Clover, an old hand at performing in front of an

audience, squirmed uncomfortably. Lady Cordial was so awkward and shy Clover's heart went out to her. Clearly she wished she was light-years away—not standing onstage, about to deliver a major announcement.

"Ahem." Lady Cordial cleared her throat. "S-s-s-s-star greetings, s-s-s-s-s-students," she stuttered.

"Do you know she s-s-s-s-s-s-s-stutters?" Vivica said in a stage whisper to Brenna.

Clover groaned to herself. Why did Lady Cordial always choose words that started with the letter *s*?

"I will get right to the point," Lady Cordial continued.

Clover nodded encouragingly at the stage. Not one S-word in that sentence! That was a start.

Lady Cordial dropped the mic, and the thud echoed throughout the room.

"S-s-s-s-s-s-star apologies!" she cried.

Clover glared around the room, daring anyone to laugh.

"I asked you here today," Lady Cordial said, plowing ahead, a bright purple blush flooding her cheeks, "to relay important news."

Clover sat forward expectantly. This definitely had to do with Lady Stella. Did Lady Cordial know what had happened to her?

"Lady S-s-s-s-s-stella has been unexpectedly called away due to a family emergency."

A loud hum filled the auditorium. *Okay*, Clover thought. *Lady Stella is really gone. And the family emergency must be an excuse.* But Lady Cordial looked like she had more to say.

"As director of admissions, I am next in line," she went on. "S-s-s-s-s-so I will be temporarily in charge."

The room erupted with cries of surprise. Only the Star Darlings remained silent, exchanging worried glances.

Lady Cordial called for quiet. She waved her arms frantically, but the noise didn't subside. Finally, Professor Dolores Raye whistled for everyone's attention, and the students settled down.

Lady Cordial nodded, as if she'd called on the teacher to step in. "I hope everyone will be patient with me. This is a huge s-s-s-s-s-step, with a definite learning curve. It may take s-s-s-s-s-some time for everything to run s-s-s-s-s-smoothly."

Three S-words, Clover thought. Not quite a record. But she knew Lady Cordial's speech would end with a great big embarrassing double-S phrase. She waited a beat, then nodded as Lady Cordial finished with "S-s-s-s-star s-s-s-s-salutations."

The lights brightened once again. The assembly was over.

The Star Darlings, in silent agreement, stayed seated while the other students hurried out, eager to talk about the news. Not even Vivica gave the "SDs" a glance.

Clover pulled Astra to her feet. "We should talk things over," she told the group. "Astra, is it okay if everyone comes to our room?"

Just then their Star-Zaps buzzed with a group holo-text. Clover read it quickly: "'Please report to Lady Stella's office immediately.'"

"What?" said Libby, confused. "But she's not here!"

Their Star-Zaps went off again. "'Correction: Lady Cordial's office, formerly Lady Stella's.'"

"That makes sense," Vega said in her practical way. "Lady Cordial's old office was so small and cramped you could barely turn around without knocking over a holo-file. At least now she'll have space to get organized."

But they found that Lady Cordial's new office was anything but organized. It looked like a lightning bolt had struck. Holo-books lay scattered on the floor. Desk drawers hung open haphazardly. And Lady Stella's lovely silver table was buried under holo-files.

Lady Cordial was nowhere to be seen.

"That's strange," said Clover, peering around. "Why would she call a meeting if she's not even here?"

"S-s-s-s-s-sit down, girls." Clover spied two feet, clad in clunky purple shoes, sticking out from under the desk. "I'll be with you in a s-s-s-s-starsec."

If Clover had been in a different frame of mind, she would have burst out laughing. She watched as Lady Cordial squirmed her way out, took a deep breath, then stumbled to her feet.

"Can we help you?" asked Cassie.

She shook her head. "I've looked everywhere. It's gone."

"What's gone?" asked Leona.

Lady Cordial sighed. "Lady S-s-s-stella had a wish energy meter that she used to determine the balance of energy. It's nowhere to be found. Sh-sh-sh-she must have taken it with her," she finished, seating herself in Lady Stella's chair.

Clover sucked in her breath. It was silly, she knew, but she wished that space could stay empty, at least until everything was straightened out.

"I wanted to sh-sh-sh-share my thoughts with you, girls. You've already told me everything that happened when you last s-s-s-s-s-saw Lady S-s-s-s-stella. Now it's my turn." Lady Cordial leaned forward, knocking over one holo-file, two holo-books, and a galliope figurine.

While she reached down to pick up the items, Clover thought back to everything that had happened.

Right after Adora had returned from her mission, the Star Darlings had agreed they needed to confront Lady Stella. But they'd decided to talk to Lady Cordial first. She'd know exactly what to do, they thought.

"Of course I told you I'd s-s-s-support you when you s-s-s-spoke to Lady S-s-s-stella," Lady Cordial said now, following Clover's swift train of thought. "Unfortunately, as you know, my sh-sh-sh-shoe got jammed in the Cosmic Transporter and I had to ride around the s-s-s-school twice, missing the meeting."

At first, Lady Stella had been pleased to see them, Clover remembered. She'd been urging them to come to her with questions or concerns. And finally, there they were. But then Cassie and Scarlet took turns talking, Cassie looking torn even as she outlined all the evidence, and Scarlet not quite meeting Lady Stella's eyes. And Lady Stella's calm expression had turned stormy.

Finally, Cassie had finished, saying, "We believe you should not be the headmistress anymore."

Lady Stella nodded slowly. "Forgive me," she said, standing up. There was a glittery flash and a crackle and pop. The air filled with smoke. When it cleared, Lady Stella was gone.

One starsec she had been there, the next she had disappeared without any explanation. Clover had been holding out hope that they were wrong. That Lady Stella would laugh and have an explanation for everything. But then Clover realized that Lady Stella must be guilty of sabotage. Why else would she run away?

Of course, that was Clover's head talking. Her heart still said something else.

"That confirms it!" Sage had said firmly as the smoke cleared, her voice only trembling a bit at the end. "Lady Stella is responsible for everything."

Lady Cordial cleared her throat, and Clover was brought back to the here (Lady Stella's office) and now (Lady Cordial in charge).

"I believe I have it all figured out," Lady Cordial said. "Lady S-s-s-stella has been training Wish-Granters for s-s-s-staryears. It is known throughout the worlds sh-sh-sh-she is the best, the brightest, the most accomplished teacher. Future Wish-Granters have thanked their lucky s-s-s-stars to be her s-s-s-s-students."

Clover nodded. She'd learned so much from Lady Stella.

"But because of her role," Lady Cordial went on, "sh-sh-sh-she was privy to knowledge the rest of us weren't privy to. For s-s-s-s-stars know how long, sh-sh-sh-she knew there was a wish energy deficit! That we'd soon be losing power. And she kept us in the dark."

"Literally," Clover joked.

"Ahem." Lady Cordial frowned, and Clover felt bad. This was hard enough for the new headmistress. She didn't need a wise-star interrupting.

"At any rate," Lady Cordial continued, "Lady S-s-s-stella eventually left a holo-letter open on her desk. I read the warnings. I confronted her, and she had to confide in me then, along with a few other faculty members. But s-s-s-still, she wasn't concerned. S-s-s-s-still she did nothing about the crisis!

"Then one s-s-s-s-starday, I was exploring the underground caves and I came upon a hidden room. It was filled with ancient tomes. I s-s-s-spent s-s-s-starhours there, poring over rare old holo-books. And then I came across a s-s-s-s-s-special one." She cast a significant look around the table. "It was about twelve S-s-s-star-Charmed S-s-s-starlings who are fated to s-s-s-s-save S-s-s-s-s-starland."

Clover bowed her head, still awed by the responsibility.

Lady Cordial continued. "I immediately realized we

could use this information to help S-s-s-s-starland. Lady S-s-s-s-s-stella was very reluctant to pursue this. But I wouldn't give up. I persevered and took matters into my own hands. I combed through records and test s-s-s-s-scores and s-s-s-sat in on classes. I identified you twelve S-s-s-s-star Darlings. Lady S-s-s-s-stella appeared to s-s-s-s-support your group. But she replaced S-s-s-s-scarlet with Ophelia for a time. She was responsible for the poisonous flowers and nail polish, for interfering with missions . . . and for trapping you in that underground room!"

"We already know all that!" Scarlet said crossly. "The question is, why? Why would she do it?"

"Lady S-s-s-s-s-stella wanted the energy deficit to worsen," Lady Cordial replied. "She was working against me . . . against us . . . against our planet . . . the whole time. Clearly, she thrives on negative energy. It gives her power. There is no other explanation." She paused. "Who knows what she would have done with that power?"

Clover gasped. Stated so baldly, it was shocking.

"What happens now?" asked Cassie.

"Excellent question. I am hoping no further action will be required. Lady S-s-s-s-s-stella must have gone into hiding. Most likely, she will never return. S-s-s-s-s-so now we work to repair the damage sh-sh-sh-she caused.

We have two Wish Missions left." Lady Cordial's eyes rested first on Clover, then on Gemma. "Much can be done."

Clover's heart thudded. Everything depended on these next missions—one of which would be hers. She'd work tirelessly to find her Wisher, to help grant the wish. And if she couldn't do it? She tossed her head to shake off doubts. It was easier said than done, but she'd just have to prove herself.

"I still can't believe it," Sage said miserably, her glow dimming. Clover knew that it was one thing to *think* Lady Stella might be evil, but it was another to have your fears confirmed.

"If you s-s-s-s-see or hear from her," Lady Cordial finished, "you must alert me immediately. Her destructive behavior cannot continue. I will not let it."

These were strong words indeed from Lady Cordial, who was usually so sweet and indecisive. Now she seemed almost fierce. All of a sudden, Clover felt glad they were on the same side.

"That is all." Lady Cordial spoke in a milder voice. "For now."

Slowly and silently, the girls filed out of the office, then left Halo Hall. Outside, they stood uneasily in a loose circle, not sure what to do next.

"We can still make it to the Celestial Café in time for a quick breakfast before class," Clover said. She didn't feel very hungry. Still, maybe the others were and would want company. But shaking their heads, sad and upset, the other girls set off in different directions.

"Tessa?" Clover called, certain that at least she would want to eat. But Tessa just turned away. Even she had lost her appetite.

CHAPTER
2

The next starday, Dododay, began in the usual way. There was breakfast, morning classes, lunch, and afternoon classes. But a shadow hung over the school. Without Lady Stella overseeing the students, everything seemed slightly off, even though on the surface nothing had changed.

So just as usual, the Star Darlings met after regular classes for their lecture.

Clover was glad to go to that class, happy to follow the regular routine and know what to expect. But deep inside she knew it wouldn't be normal at all. Lady Stella wouldn't lead the lecture or introduce a guest professor.

"It all seems so strange without Lady Stella," Clover said quietly, sliding into a seat next to Adora. "And sad."

Leona crossed her arms. "Well, I think it's all for the best. At least now we know what's what."

"Knowing and feeling are two very different things," Piper said, her eyes half-closed in meditation.

Those were almost exactly Clover's thoughts!

"Well, I know *and* feel one thing for certain," Clover said jokingly. "Lady Cordial is not going to get up in front of this class and lecture us like Lady Stella sometimes did. She's an administrator, not a teacher. We'll definitely have guest lecturers from here on."

Everyone turned to the door expectantly.

"Well, whoever it is, is late," Scarlet said.

Starmins ticked by, and still no teacher came to the room.

"Maybe our lecturer is stuck somewhere," Clover said, thinking of the stalled circus swift train. "Energy outages are everywhere."

"It's true," Libby agreed. "My parents canceled their vacation when their hotel lost its fifty-star rating because of slow service. Meals were delayed because of faulty micro-zaps, and beach towels at the cabana stand weren't dried properly."

Libby blushed a bright pink shade, realizing she came off as a bit entitled. Of course, it wasn't her fault her family was wealthy!

"We know you're not spoiled, Libby," Clover said gently.

Libby smiled gratefully and continued. "Everyone has to tighten their belts now and start conserving energy. My parents said things are pretty awful, even though the holo-papers have been downplaying the crisis. And they're not just talking about wet towels! Businesses are closing."

"Well, the only thing we can do is go about *our* business." Clover smiled at her play on words, even though no one else noticed. "Just keep collecting energy to help save Starland. Hopefully, a Wish Orb will be ready soon, and Gemma or I can go on a mission."

Then she turned to Sage. "What does your mom think?"

Sage's mother was a wish energy scientist and would be sure to know the latest news.

"I don't really know." Sage shook her head and her long lavender hair swung back and forth. "Every time we start to talk, her Star-Zap goes off and she has to take a holo-call, or she's called into a meeting. I've only gotten a few holo-texts. You know, typical mom stuff: do you need a new toothlight . . . holo-call your brothers . . ."

"Well, I'm going to holo-call my family right now,"

Leona said with a huff, "instead of sitting here and waiting for a teacher who isn't going to show."

"Yes!" Scarlet stood and stomped to the door in her heavy black boots. "Class dismissed!"

Stardays passed without any Star Darlings classes and without a Wish Orb notification from Lady Cordial. Increasingly, lights flickered and devices slowed. Still, Clover kept to her regular routine: writing songs before breakfast, going to class, and working on a big Golden Days project. It was an oral history assignment, and Clover was collecting stories from older family members.

She'd just holo-interviewed her great-uncle Octavius, who'd been a wee Starling during the Great Circus Disaster of '08. He'd described how the train's creature car had hurtled into a deep lake and everyone had jumped in to rescue the galliopes and glions. The story had a happy ending. The creatures had all survived. And there was an amusing bit about her great-uncle losing his pants.

But somehow, Clover's story kept turning into a piece about loss and disappointment. Usually, her written projects had a few jokes or witty sayings thrown in for entertainment. Now, worrying about Lady Stella and the power outages, she couldn't manage it.

At dinner that night, the overhead lights turned off and on and no even glanced up. It was becoming alarmingly routine.

"Are you done with that noddlenoodle soup?" Tessa was asking Libby hopefully. Noddlenoodle was the special of the day, and Libby had just started to slurp the one extremely long noodle in the dish. It wound round and round the bowl and could take starmins to finish. Libby, still working on the noodle, could only shake her head.

Disappointed, Tessa turned to Clover. "Don't even think about it!" Clover joked, placing her arms protectively over her own dish. "Just ask a Bot-Bot for your own soup!" She pointed out several Bot-Bot waiters hovering throughout the café, taking orders and serving meals.

"Well," said Tessa with a harrumph. "I just wanted a taste. But if you insist . . ." She waved to a nearby Bot-Bot, on its way to deliver another bowl of noddlenoodle. The Bot-Bot paused to say, "I'll be right back, Miss Tessa." Then its eyes opened wide. A loud whirring sounded from somewhere in its body, and its feet moved uselessly back and forth.

"Uh-oh," it said in its robotic voice. "I . . . am . . . about . . . to . . . power . . . down." It sank, tilting crazily. The bowl tipped over.

"No!" cried Tessa as the soup poured into her lap, the noddlenoodle winding up in a coil on her head.

The Bot-Bot, now on the floor, its face blank, had nothing to say.

"Well, there you have it," Clover said with a giggle. "Your own bowl of noddlenoodle."

And then, thanks to self-cleaning technology, the soup and noodle disappeared, leaving Tessa's skirt dry and clean, her head free of the noddlenoodle crown. Even she had to laugh.

For once, they'd found something funny about the power failures. But Clover's good mood didn't last. That night she couldn't take a sparkle shower; for the first time ever, the sparkles had run out. And she realized her Star-Zap had failed to record her Wishling Ways lecture, so she couldn't study while she slept.

Everyone was complaining about power problems early the next day, Yumday, as Clover and the Star Darlings joined the rest of the school for the weekly assembly.

"I bet we'll talk about the energy crisis," Gemma predicted.

"It would be hard to ignore," Tessa agreed.

"Unless Lady Cordial wants everything to seem as normal as possible," Clover said. "Then there'd just be the regular announcements and presentations."

Sure enough, Lady Cordial stumbled onstage and began the assembly with the traditional Starlandian Pledge of Illumination, same as usual. She then recited a long list of updates: students celebrating Bright Days, a holo–book club meeting, a special presentation by the drama club.

"Don't miss out on that," Lady Cordial said, nodding approvingly. "It includes a holo-retrospective of their most talented alumna, a student named Cora, who s-s-s-specialized in villainous roles."

Lady Cordial went on and on until she came to the last order of business: a demonstration by the Ultimate Frisbeam club. The girls walked onstage, holding their disks of light, ready to perform.

A loud voice interrupted the assembly: "Starscuse me, students!" The Frisbeam team stopped, confused. "I don't mean to interfere with your performance, girls. But the assembly is drawing to a close, and we still haven't discussed a topic of utmost importance: the energy crisis."

A tall, thin imposing figure rose from the first row of teachers. Her bright red hair framed her narrow face like a sun's corona. "It's that new teacher!" Astra hissed to Clover. "Professor Honoria McHue. She just took over my Astronomics class."

The teacher stood, half facing the audience, half turned toward Lady Cordial and the stage.

She certainly has everyone's attention, Clover thought admiringly. All the students were sitting up straight now, alert and interested.

Lady Cordial stared at Professor Honoria McHue, flustered.

"What exactly is being done here?" the teacher demanded. "I've heard other schools have started conserving energy. Is that an option at Starling Academy?"

Lady Cordial nodded so vigorously her bun came loose. "Of course it is, Professor Honoria McHue. I was planning on addressing the issue, of course—at a more appropriate time. But I will get right to it now. I feel the best course of action is to establish committees to research those options."

While Lady Cordial continued, the students settled back in their seats. Scarlet yawned.

"Each committee can be tailored to focus on one aspect of the issue," Lady Cordial went on, "s-s-s-s-so the eventual plan will be s-s-s-s-stronger as a whole. For instance, the Rules and Regulations Committee can be headed by Professor Dolores Raye." Lady Cordial took a few steps toward the professor, as if to introduce her, and tripped over her own feet. She tumbled to the ground with a loud thud. "Oh, my s-s-s-s-stars!" she cried, holding her ankle. "Can s-s-s-s-someone call an EMB?"

The assembly ended in chaos. Emergency Medical Bot-Bots rushed to Lady Cordial's aid. But many didn't have the energy to reach the stage. They slowed, then stopped, blocking the aisles.

Finally, the Bot-Bots were rebooted. They carried Lady Cordial out on a stretcher and flew her to the infirmary. The assembly was officially over. Slowly, moving with the crowd, the Star Darlings made their way to the starmarble lobby.

"Should we just go to lunch?" Tessa asked the others. "It's early, but the café is open. If we're the first ones there, the Bot-Bots will still have plenty of energy to serve us."

"That makes sense," said Clover. They turned toward the Cosmic Transporter just as all their Star-Zaps went off.

"I have a feeling this is important," Piper murmured. She patted her pockets, then went through her big green bag, taking out a sleep mask, a dream journal, and other odds and ends as she searched for her device.

Clover watched Piper with amusement. She wasn't the most organized Starling around. Clover, on the other hand, liked to be fully prepared—always.

"Ready when you are" was, in fact, the credo of the Flying Molensas. The family was constantly on the go, with all their belongings in tow. *Hmmm*, thought Clover, *nice rhyme.* Maybe she could use it in a song.

Then she flicked her Star-Zap and read the message aloud to share with Piper. "'To all faculty and students.'"

"It's from Professor Honoria McHue!" Piper said, looking over her shoulder. "She sent a holo-mail blast to the whole school."

Nodding, Clover continued reading: "'Every Starling—here at the academy and across the planet—should be asking questions about the state of our energy supply. Why have there been power outages? Our energy is supposed to be continuously replenished! Are our Wish-Houses in order? Is negative energy affecting our Wish Orbs? And what can we do about our wish energy manipulation losing its power? If you have suggestions or would like to discuss any of these points, I am available. Starfully yours, Professor Honoria McHue.'"

"That's hitting the starnail on the head," said Scarlet, reading over the holo-mail on her own Star-Zap. She flicked to a news site. "And listen to this. *The Daily Moon* reports major outages in Solar Springs and Gloom Flats."

Tessa and Gemma were from Solar Springs; Piper was from Gloom Flats. *This is really hitting close to home*, Clover thought.

The sisters bent over their Star-Zaps, tapping furiously. A starsec later, Tessa and Gemma heard back from their mom. Gemma read the quick holo-text out loud. "'All farm creatures are fine. Hydro-energy system not working, so crops may be in danger. Garble greens in bad shape.'"

"No loss there!" Clover joked. Hardly anyone enjoyed eating the bitter green vegetable—except for Tessa. "Sorry, Tessa."

"'But Dad and I found some antique watering cans,'" Gemma continued, "'so don't worry!'"

Piper, meanwhile, had finally found her Star-Zap and sent off her own holo-text. "Oh," she groaned. "It keeps bouncing back. I can't get through!"

Piper's grandmother and brother lived in such an out-of-the-way place that their lines of communication were probably the first to go, Clover thought.

Piper took a deep breath, closed her eyes, and seemed to go to a different place for a moment. Clover had seen this happen before. So had all the other Star Darlings. They waited patiently.

"It's all right," Piper said, opening her eyes. "Gran is sending messages our old-fashioned family way. And mind-mail never fails! She and my brother are both fine."

"That's good," Clover said, relieved. Then she was filled with determination. "But we need to help any way we can—Wish Orb or no Wish Orb. We are the Star-Charmed Starlings."

Everyone nodded. Clover knew she sounded sure and in control. But what could they do without Lady Stella's guidance? They were just students, after all. And some were just first years, away from home for the very first time. Were they really prepared to take on Starland's fate?

Yes, she decided.

But maybe Lady Cordial was wondering the same thing! Maybe she was hesitant to send them on a mission.

"We need to see Lady Cordial," Clover told the others. "To the infirmary!"

CHAPTER
3

Clover, always in good health, had barely stepped foot in the Interstellar Infirmary during her two staryears at school. Now she noted the floor glistened with extra starpolish. A strong but not unpleasant antiseptic smell floated through the air.

She led the Star Darlings to the front desk. Smiling at the receptionist, she said warmly, "We're here to see Lady Cordial."

"Well," said the Starling, smiling back, "that's nice."

"Yes," said Clover pleasantly. "What room is she in?"

"I can't tell you that," the receptionist said, still smiling. "Lady Cordial has requested privacy. No visitors allowed."

Surely Lady Cordial didn't mean the Star Darlings! The receptionist had to let them in. Clover was doing her best to establish a bond with the woman—just like she'd been taught as a performer—smiling, speaking with friendly good humor. It seemed to be working. So she'd give it another try.

"I know Lady Cordial would be pleased to see us," Clover told the receptionist. If only they'd brought flowers—calliopes or chatterbursts. That would convince the woman.

"Take a seat," the receptionist said, waving toward the waiting area. "Lady Cordial is with the doctor. I'll see what I can do later. But right now I am swamped with work."

She whirled around to face a holo-keyboard, then examined her nails one by one.

"I guess we'll wait," Clover said, disappointed. Nodding, the girls sat down. Some flipped through old holo-magazines. Leona snickered, looking at the cover of *Starlebrity Journal*. "Look at this actor. He's so last staryear."

While everyone else crowded around, Clover decided to explore. In case the receptionist didn't follow through, she wanted to find Lady Cordial's room. She sidled down the hall, tiptoeing past empty rooms, until she heard voices in one room. She peeked through the door.

"We can't find anything wrong with you," a doctor was saying, her back blocking Clover's view. "But since you are in such pain . . ."

"Yes," said Lady Cordial in such a weak voice that Clover had to strain to hear. "I am in a great deal of pain."

"We'll keep you overnight for observation." The doctor turned and left. Clover jumped back, not wanting Lady Cordial to spot her. But it was too late.

Starf! thought Clover. What if Lady Cordial really didn't want to see them? Clover had gone and put her in an awkward position. And Lady Cordial wasn't at her best in difficult situations.

"Clover," Lady Cordial said falteringly, "you've come to s-s-s-s-see me."

"We all have, Lady Cordial, if that's okay."

"Yes," Lady Cordial said with a sigh. "But just for a few s-s-s-s-starmins. I don't have much s-s-s-s-s-strength."

Clover hurried to get the other Star Darlings and they all squeezed into the room.

Lady Cordial lay in bed, the sheet pulled up to her chin.

"How are you feeling?" asked Tessa. "Is it your ankle?"

Lady Cordial shook her head wearily. "At first I thought it was, but now I'm not s-s-s-so sure. The s-s-s-s-staff is running tests. It could be s-s-s-s-serious."

Maybe keeping someone for observation meant running tests. And "we can't find anything wrong with you" meant the doctor didn't want to frighten poor Lady Cordial.

Clover's glow flared with remorse. *We should have been visiting Lady Cordial because it's the right thing to do,* she told herself, *not because of our energy crisis.* But they were there now. So they might as well proceed.

Lady Cordial closed her eyes.

Clover edged closer to the bed. She'd better say something fast! "Since we're here," she said, "we thought we could talk about energy. We're hearing all sorts of reports about power outages."

"And it's been so long since we've had a mission," Cassie said.

"Yes," Clover said. "Maybe you're worried about Gemma or me not being ready, so you're holding off on sending us. But there's no need to worry. You can trust us."

Lady Cordial said nothing. She began to breathe evenly. Was she sleeping? Should they leave?

Then Scarlet stepped forward, bumping into the bed. Lady Cordial's eyelids fluttered a bit.

"It would be a very good time for a Wish Mission," Scarlet told her loudly. "Lady Stella isn't here to sabotage us. So we should be able to collect a starmendous amount of wish energy." She smiled. "I wish I could go back again. I really liked it on Wishworld."

"We can check the orbs!" Clover offered, thinking quickly. "Since you're in the infirmary, we can monitor them and see if one is ready."

Lady Cordial's eyes snapped open.

"Oh, good!" cried Leona. "Our visit is helping. You look wide awake now."

"S-s-s-s-sweet of you," Lady Cordial murmured, half closing her eyes again. "But I can keep track of the orbs remotely." She gestured at her Star-Zap on the nightstand, and it fell to the floor with a clatter.

Clover picked it up and put it out of Lady Cordial's reach, just for safekeeping. "I wish we could do something!"

"Maybe you can," said Lady Cordial. "I, too, have been following the reports." Her voice grew louder, as if relating her idea was giving her strength. "All the heads of s-s-s-s-schools are comparing notes on the energy crisis. I just heard about one s-s-s-s-school at the top of Mount Glint where they are making their own alternative fuel source. I don't know any details. But perhaps you girls could look into it? I can write you a s-s-s-s-starscuse note for missing class tomorrow. Why not take a trip and check it out?"

"That would be starmazing!" Sage said. "So we won't just be waiting for the Wish Orb!" She smiled at Clover. "Like you said, we'll be doing something!"

"Yes, something any old Starling could do," said Scarlet. "We should be concentrating on collecting wish energy. Remember, we're the chosen ones."

"And Mount Glint is so far away." Leona frowned. "It's really quite a hike."

"Oh, come now," said Lady Cordial. "You twelve are s-s-s-star-charmed. But who knows what fate has in s-s-s-store for you? What role the S-s-s-s-star Darlings will need to take?"

Piper nodded, and a dreamy expression crossed her face. Clover knew what would happen next. Piper would recount a dream and interpret it.

"I did just have a dream," Piper said, her forehead furrowed in concentration. "I was walking . . . walking . . . I couldn't tell where I was going. But I wasn't alone. And I needed to reach a specific destination. The fate of Starland depended on it."

She shook her head to clear it. "Maybe it means we should travel to Mount Glint."

"Well, count me out," Scarlet said crossly. "It doesn't make sense."

"I'm with Scarlet." Leona linked arms with her roommate. Clover blinked. More and more often lately, the two roommates—universes apart in every way—were in agreement. It was odd to see, but really nice. "It sounds like a lot of work and no payoff," Leona continued.

"But we all need to be together," Clover argued. "The oracle states clearly there are twelve Star-Charmed Starlings. Not ten." She looked at Cassie, the only Star Darling the other two would listen to. "Right?"

"We do need to stick together," Cassie agreed. "In the ancient book, the energy at the center of the holo-drawing comes from all of us working together."

"Yes!" Gemma grabbed Tessa's hand. "We stick together!"

Lady Cordial leaned back, looking exhausted.

"We'll go tomorrow," Clover said quickly, before Scarlet or Leona could say anything else. "And we should leave you, Lady Cordial, so you can rest."

Lady Cordial lifted her hand in a feeble wave. "Farewell and s-s-s-star s-s-s-speed," she said drowsily.

Walking on tiptoe, the girls filed out of the room.

"And bring your S-s-s-s-star Darlings backpacks," Lady Cordial called out in a surprisingly loud voice, "in case you need to carry the energy s-s-s-s-source back!"

Early the next starday, just as the moons were eclipsed by the suns, the girls met between the two dorms. They'd all had a bit of difficulty getting ready. Their manipulation energy was slowing down, and sparkle showers took forever to sparkle. But there they were, everyone except Clover and Gemma carrying a backpack as Lady Cordial had instructed.

Tessa handed out astromuffins, saying, "I hear Mount Glint's cafeteria can't hold a hololight to ours. So just in case we get hungry . . ."

"Star salutations," Vega said, placing the muffin in her backpack. "Now," she said, turning to Clover, "are you sure you have the route figured out? I checked some holo-maps and—"

"Vega! I said I could do it!" Clover interrupted. "We just take a few hover-buses, then walk a bit." She consulted her Star-Zap holo-map. "We can get the first one right at the gate. It's the number twelve bus."

"Twelve!" said Piper, delighted. "A wonderful sign."

And it did seem to be a sign. The bus was already at the stop, as if waiting just for them. The door lifted.

"No passengers!" the Bot-Bot said, hurriedly closing the door without further explanation.

The bus didn't move, and the girls stood there impatiently. "Maybe it will take us after all," Libby said hopefully. But then a sign on the side of the bus flashed: OUT OF SERVICE. OUT OF POWER.

"When will the next one come?" Adora asked.

"Right now," Clover said, pointing down the street. But that one was so crowded the Bot-Bot conductor poked its head out and said, "No room!" before the bus sped away.

A starhour later, the girls finally boarded the first bus, which was by then fully functional. "So," Clover said, checking the map, "we change buses at Starland City Hall."

"Starland City Hall?" Vega blinked. "We could have walked there!"

In no time at all, the Star Darlings reached Starland City Hall and changed buses, first to the number 593, then to the number .003, and finally to the number 6,672.

"Now, this one will take us right to the foot of Mount Glint!" Clover said triumphantly.

"If we ever get there," said Adora as the bus sputtered to a stop.

"We are having problems with the power steering," the Bot-Bot conductor announced. "All passengers must disembark. Another bus will arrive in one starhour."

Two starhours later, the girls finally reached their destination: the foot of Mount Glint. Clover gazed at her friends. They all looked grumpy and tired. And they still had to hike up the mountain!

"This way," Clover said cheerfully, leading them to a path. "We're almost there!" she added, though she really had no idea.

Luckily, Mount Glint turned out to be more of a hill than a mountain, and the path was smooth and wide. Still feeling responsible, though, Clover made up a marching song to energize the group.

Left, right, left right—
We're almost there, we're on our way.
Right, left. Right left—
Right in the middle of a star school day.

Before Clover knew it, they'd reached the top, having stopped only once, to eat Tessa's astromuffins. The suns were shining brightly, the grass sparkled with glow-dew, and multicolored glittery trees swayed in the breeze. Clover's spirits rose.

The girls walked a few steps more to a narrow walkway, which was marked with a sign: WELCOME TO THE MOUNT GLINT SCHOOL, WHERE LEARNING IS SUNDAMENTAL.

The path led directly to the campus, built on a much smaller scale than Starling Academy. Its low one-story buildings seemed a bit worn.

"They don't have a Cosmic Transporter?" Libby asked.

"I think we're on it," Scarlet said. "It's just not working."

"They must be restructuring it for the new energy source," Clover said determinedly. "Maybe they've discovered that energy can come from those colorful trees we passed."

"Or from that dirt road we took!" Scarlet smirked.

Clover sighed. Of course her guess was just a moonshot. And usually she was the one with the sarcastic one-liner. But if she dished it out, she had to take it, so she just grinned.

"Okay, enough joking around," Scarlet said, actually returning the smile. "I don't want to waste another starsec on this silly trip. . . . Starscuse me," she said, stopping an official-looking adult with large glasses on top of her head, holding back her dark green hair. "Can you tell us anything about an alternative energy source?"

The woman looked at her, baffled.

"Or at least direct us to the head of the school," Clover added quickly, not giving up. "She'd know what we're talking about."

"I am the head of the school, Lady Marissa."

"Star greetings, Lady Marissa," Clover said, politely bowing her head. "We're from Starling Academy. And we heard your school is using a new energy source. But we don't have any other details."

"That's because there are no details—and no energy source," the headmistress said. "I did send a holo-mail to headmasters and -mistresses across Starland, suggesting we spearhead a research effort. But no one thought I was serious. In fact, they thought I was joking. Here." She showed Clover the reply from Star Prep's headmaster, which Clover read aloud.

"'Star salutations for the laugh. If only laughter could be used for fuel, I would show your holo-letter to everyone.'"

Everyone's a comedian, Clover thought grimly.

Lady Marissa sighed. "I guess he's right. Our history holo-books tell us the founding Starlings tried everything before they stumbled upon wish-granting energy."

Clover sighed along with her. How disappointing. She hated to go back and tell Lady Cordial the bad news.

"And as you can probably tell," Lady Marissa continued, waving an arm to indicate the dim campus, "we are on energy rationing right now, saving our resources for overcast days and nights."

Clover nodded. Lady Marissa was trying to be helpful. Unfortunately, she couldn't give them what they wanted: a way to save Starland. "Star salutations anyway," Clover said as the Star Darlings began to retrace their steps. Now they'd have to make the long trip back empty-handed. Everyone was grumbling unhappily.

"Look on the bright side," Scarlet said, nudging her as they walked. "I see a Starcab stand right over there. There are three cabs hovering, so we can divide up into groups of four and just drive home.

"I have only one question for you, circus star: why didn't we do this in the first place?"

Even with Starcabs, the trip back wasn't easy; the cabs had to stop to recharge again and again. Finally, as the first stars began to shine, the Star Darlings walked through the school gates, just in time for dinner. The girls ate quickly, then decided to go to the infirmary and tell Lady Cordial what had happened.

Unfortunately, it seemed the stars were still against them. Lady Cordial had checked out. They hurried to her office, but she wasn't there, either.

Clover felt terrible hauling everyone all over campus—especially after dragging them all around Starland. "I'll go to her house," she told the others. "Everyone else should just go to bed."

Walking alone, Clover made her way to the faculty

residences. She placed her hand on a scanner and walked through the entrance as the curtain of leaves slowly parted.

Clover recognized Lady Cordial's house immediately. The teachers' homes looked just like them. And Lady Cordial's was the same shade of purple as her hair, with an unkempt yard and a frazzled look. Clover strode to the door and knocked loudly.

She looked up and saw the curtains on the second floor ripple slightly, as if someone was peering out. But she must have been mistaken. Lady Cordial didn't answer the door.

I probably just missed her, Clover thought, disappointed. Maybe now she was back at her office, catching up on work.

Clover sighed. Another wasted trip. Quickly, she turned to walk up the overgrown path. *Wait, what was that?*

A newish home a little farther up the street had caught her attention. It was tall and narrow, imposing and no-nonsense, with a bright red roof and a silvery sheen.

That must be Professor Honoria McHue's house, Clover told herself. *I'm here. I might as well talk to her.*

The teacher had raised so many interesting questions;

maybe she actually had answers, too. But just as Clover reached the front steps, a holo-sign appeared.

ATTENTION, VISITORS! PROFESSOR HONORIA MCHUE HAS TAKEN A POSITION AT A WEE STARLINGS SCHOOL IN GLOOM FLATS, EFFECTIVE IMMEDIATELY. HER STARLING ACADEMY HOLO-MAIL HAS BEEN DISCONTINUED, AND THERE IS NO FORWARDING ADDRESS. WE WISH HER ALL THE BEST!

Well, that was sudden, Clover thought. She hoped the teacher was happier at her new job, but her absence certainly didn't help the situation at Starling Academy.

Standing by the leaf curtain a starmin later, she flicked her wrist to open the exit. Nothing happened. She was too low on energy to use her manipulation skills—that was the problem. Groaning a bit, Clover pushed her way through.

Would things keep getting worse?

Clover wasn't the only Star Darling who was worried. It seemed everyone's spirits were so dim that the sparkle had gone out of their eyes . . . and hair . . . and skin. And of course that was perfectly understandable. Nothing was going right.

Clover had eventually found Lady Cordial, to tell her about the Mount Glint fiasco. But the new headmistress, while feeling better, was too busy catching up on work to come up with more suggestions. Plus there was still no sign of a Wish Orb. Add to that the worthless, time-consuming trip to Mount Glint, and Clover felt her own energy level sink.

She felt responsible for cheering everyone up. *And what makes every Starling smile?* she asked herself. *A circus, of course!*

Excited by the idea, Clover sat at her desk to holo-type some notes. The atmosphere had to be fun and daring, bright and energetic. For starters, she could give star-swallowing lessons. She made a note: *order at least twelve stars.* And she'd need a cloud candy machine. What was a circus without that fluffy, sticky, sweet treat on a stick?

Then she had another idea. There was a galliope stable a couple of floozels away. She could bring over a few and work up a routine—standing on one galliope's back while it galloped, then leaping to another and swinging from the tip of its glowing tail to its sparkly mane.

Clover's mind raced with more plans. *Juggling! A clown act!* She could set up a starwire between trees. She could use the school's trampoline for a tumbling performance!

Clover designed a flyer announcing the circus to the Star Darlings: COME ONE, COME ALL! COME TO THE SHORES OF LUMINOUS LAKE AND SEE THE GREATEST SHOW AT STARLING ACADEMY! She added a date and time and grinned. It would be starmazing!

Next Clover placed orders for the cloud candy machine, the galliopes, the special starwire, and more. But the holo-request for the machine never went through. Another energy blip. The galliopes were already booked for a wee Starling's Bright Day party. And when the starwire came, Clover realized it was all wrong. The company had accidentally sent a firewire, a replacement part for micro-zaps!

How could she tell everyone the circus was canceled? She couldn't. The day of the big event, she trudged to Luminous Lake. Any starmin everyone would arrive, and all she had were some star balls to juggle and clown makeup and accessories her mom had sent by lightning delivery.

Clover was going to let everyone down—again. The circus would have proven she could do something besides lead them on wild glowgoose chases for energy. She'd been waiting and waiting for a chance to make a difference—to go on her own Wish Mission, to be a true Star Darling. And now she wasn't even a true circus performer.

"Hello, Clover." Piper appeared out of nowhere. "Where's the circus?"

Clover bit her lip. "You're looking at it."

"Really?" Astra said, walking over with the others. She kicked a star ball to Clover. Automatically, Clover ducked under the ball so it landed on her head. The ball spun around twice, then dropped into her waiting hands.

"That's starrific! Can you do more tricks?" Sage asked.

"Of course she can!" Astra said encouragingly.

So Clover juggled all the star balls. She bounced them off trees, off a fence, and even off the lake with a bit of energy manipulation. Then she showed everyone else how to do it, too. Soon all the Star Darlings were laughing and participating.

Meanwhile, Leona wandered over to the clown supplies and started playing around. Before Clover knew it, all the girls had big glowing noses and twinkling stars painted around their eyes, and were wearing suspenders and giant shoes. They pushed each other around playfully, tripped over their big feet, and tossed buckets of starfetti, pretending it was water.

Finally, they collapsed on the ground in fits of giggles. "That was more fun than Light Giving Day!" Libby said, still laughing. And everyone agreed.

Later that starnight, lying in her hammock, Clover couldn't fall asleep. She was very glad the circus had turned out so well. Who would have thought that star balls and clown makeup could be just as much fun as a three-star circus! But still, she felt like the event had been missing something—or someone.

Lady Stella.

Clover knew Lady Stella—or the Lady Stella she remembered, anyway—would have been pleased that everyone had fun and proud of Clover for pulling it off against the odds.

Clover had been close to giving up, just like when she had first come to school and had a starmendously tough homework assignment. It was a project for her Wish Energy Manipulation class, and the deadline was looming.

She was new to Starling Academy, and expectations couldn't have been too high. But Clover wanted to prove herself right away. She'd already spent starhours tinkering around with ideas for a basic manipulation demonstration. The assignment was to use a starsack of groceries. But the assorted fruits and vegetables were just so uninteresting! And she couldn't come up with anything special. So she'd moved to a picnic table outside the Illumination Library, hoping for a fresh perspective.

At the table, she'd set her Star-Zap to record. She was ready to take a holo-video to hand in. But ozziefruit? Garble greens? Plantannas? Dull, dull, dull.

The bag stood there doing nothing, totally uninspiring. She looked at it through narrowed eyes. Should she transfer the food onto dishes? Boring. Separate the groceries into food groups? Glo-hum.

"I can't do this!" she'd said out loud.

"Clover?" Lady Stella had said, gliding over in her graceful way. "Are you having trouble with homework?"

"Um." Clover was at a loss for words. The headmistress was so lovely and kind, and of course Clover wanted to impress her. But she couldn't even speak. All her circus training, and she was starstruck!

Finally, she'd managed to tell Lady Stella the problem. It helped to look into her eyes and feel her concern.

"Well," Lady Stella had said, "what's the worst that could happen with this project?"

"I'd get a D for Dim or G for Gloomy."

"I'd say the worst thing would be if you ate all the food and couldn't do the assignment at all."

Was Lady Stella kidding around? Clover couldn't be sure. But she felt her shoulders relax.

As if she'd read her mind, Lady Stella said, "I'm trying to help you relax, Clover, because I think you need to figure out a fun approach. I hear you like to joke around."

"Is that a good thing?" Clover asked.

Lady Stella smiled. "You make people laugh and you lift their spirits. Of course that's a good thing. Perhaps you can add more of your personality to the project."

While Lady Stella waited patiently, Clover thought about the groceries, funny things she could do with the items, and what would make her laugh if she was watching it on holo-video.

Finally, she took one plantanna—a curved tubelike glowing yellow fruit. She placed it on the table. Then she stepped away and, using her wish energy manipulation skills, peeled it completely in one long motion. Slowly, she guided the peel to the ground.

Whistling nonchalantly now, Clover walked closer to the plantanna, into the video frame. "Whoa!" she cried, slipping on the skin. She flew through the air, twisted her body into a flip, and landed with her feet solidly on the ground.

"Was that a-*peeling*?" Clover joked.

Lady Stella laughed and clapped. "I believe you nailed it, Clover."

Clover had, in fact, received an I for Illumination on the project, and her holo-vid was the hit of the class. Right after, she'd run to Lady Stella's office to show her the grade. The headmistress had been as delighted as Clover, repeatedly saying how proud she was of her.

But had Lady Stella really been proud and delighted? Or had she been pretending? How could someone who seemed so supportive, kind, and open have been secretly plotting against her students?

A purple-tinted tear trickled down Clover's cheek. It was all so very sad.

CHAPTER 5

"**Come on, Clover!** You're supposed to be lighting me up for the game! Not bringing me down."

"I know, Astra! I know! Star apologies!"

Clover and Astra were on their way to a special star ball game, held at night, under the stars. It was the Glowin' Glions versus their biggest rival, the Bright Horizons. Astra had asked Clover to walk over early with her, to help her drum up some energy.

Clover knew she wasn't doing a very good job. But now she was outside on a beautiful evening. The temperature was a mild ten degrees Starrius, and the stars twinkled brightly. Rainstorms were called for later. But if everything proceeded on time, the game should be over well before they hit.

And really, rain was a good thing, Clover remembered. With hydration machines not working properly, crops were drying out. But right then Clover wanted to push any thoughts about the energy shortage out of her mind. It felt good to look forward to a night of pure enjoyment.

"You'll knock those players' starsocks off!" Clover said encouragingly. "Who's the best? Astra's the best!" she cheered loudly.

Astra grinned. "That's way better."

Together, the roommates walked to the locker room, where Clover gave Astra a quick hug for good luck.

"Remember when all you did was hug me?" Astra said with a smile. "That was starmazingly annoying."

Clover smiled back. Her odd behavior—caused by the poisonous nail polish—seemed like ancient history. So much had happened between then and now. "Tell you what," she told Astra. "If you win—which I'm sure you will—I promise *not* to hug you!"

Astra disappeared between the rows of brightly colored lockers while Clover made her way to the stadium. It was still early. The stands were empty; Clover had her choice of seats.

She walked to the midfield, then up a number of

rows so she'd have a perfect view of the action. Then she counted off eleven seats, reserving ten for the other Star Darlings, and settled into one at the end. Immediately, it transformed into a swift train seat, the most comfortable chair Clover could imagine—one that always made her feel at home.

Slowly, the other seats filled up. In ones, twos, and threes, the rest of the Star Darlings arrived. A nervous-looking Cassie, clutching a large bag at her side, slipped in beside Clover, and the stadium seat turned into a reading chair, complete with headrest. Leona, next to Cassie, sat regally on a padded golden throne.

The stadium was packed now, every seat taken.

Shaking her head, Leona leaned over Cassie to complain to Clover. "Can you believe I won't be singing—I mean *no one* will be singing—the Starlandian anthem? They're just having a parade of athletes. Like that's appropriate!" She opened her glittery cropped blazer to reveal a microphone in an inside pocket. "I brought it along just in case there's a change in plans," she confided.

Cassie, meanwhile, kept looking inside the bag. Clover thought, *She has glow-ants in her pants*, as her great-uncle Octavius used to say.

"Are you okay?" Clover whispered.

Cassie nodded and closed the top of the bag, a guilty look on her face. "I just can't seem to settle down. I think it's because I miss Lady Stella."

"I know," Clover said sympathetically.

"I mean, I believed she was guilty. I guess I still do. The evidence is overwhelming. That's why I pushed everyone to confront her. But Starling Academy just seems wrong without her."

Cassie stopped talking as the teams ran onto the field for warm-ups. A cheer rose from the fans. Libby held up a holo-sign that read GLOW, GLOWIN' GLIONS! GLOW, ASTRA!

Thirty starmins passed, then forty, then fifty. The players were still stretching and taking practice kicks. "Why isn't it starting?" Cassie asked.

"We must be waiting for Lady Cordial," Clover said. "The headmistress always *kicks* off the games." She looked at Cassie to see if she got the joke. But Cassie was rearranging her bag again and hadn't heard.

Thirty more starmins ticked by; then an announcer said: "Attention, fans! Lady Cordial, head of Starling Academy, will now welcome the athletes and lead the parade."

And finally, there she was, on the field, in front of

the crowd, looking anxious and frazzled. The two teams lined up on either side of her.

"Oh, my stars," said Leona. "She's tucked the back of her skirt into her stockings."

Clover saw that sure enough, Lady Cordial's rumpled skirt was hiked up in a very unflattering way.

Leona started waving at Astra and finally got her attention. She pointed to Lady Stella. Astra shrugged, then took a closer look. Her mouth, in an O of surprise, said it all.

"S-s-s-s-s-star apologies for the delay in getting s-s-s-started," Lady Cordial said into a microphone. "It s-s-s-seems I had the wrong time on my S-s-s-s-star-Zap. But now—"

Astra had edged around the athletes, moving in back of the line until she reached Lady Cordial. Now she was whispering urgently in her ear.

Clover heard a loud gasp. Lady Cordial reached behind her to fix her skirt, and Astra slipped back into place.

"But now," Lady Cordial continued, her glow flaring with embarrassment, "I'd like to introduce the teams."

Somehow she got through the names, bungling only the longer ones and calling Astra Adora by mistake.

Finally, sighing with relief, she led the procession in an awkward but uneventful march around the field. With a wave at the audience, she took a seat behind the team bench.

"I'm glad that's over," Clover told Cassie. "But at least Lady Cordial remembered the game!"

The referee flashed a holo-star, and the teams got into position on the field. Another holo-star signaled the start.

Astra passed the star ball back to a defender, then sprinted forward, waving her arms to show she was open. She used her wish energy manipulation to control the ball, then raced toward the goal. The Brights' goalie bounced on her toes, ready to stop the shot. But Astra concentrated the ball high and into the corner of the net—impossible to deflect. Goal for the Glions! The crowd roared.

By the end of the second half, the Brights had come back with two goals, while the Glions had added one more. The score was tied. Now a girl on the Brights had the star ball and was making a run up the field.

Cassie gripped Clover's hand. "It's almost over!" she said, excited. "If they make this goal, the Glions won't have time for another attempt!"

The player was closing in on the net, with a clear

path ahead and no defender close by. Suddenly, the field lights sputtered out. Gasps and cries of surprise erupted throughout the stadium. The game came to a standstill.

The referee flashed a star. "Startime out!" she called. "Spectators, please set your Star-Zaps on flashlight mode so the game can continue."

They all pulled out their Star-Zaps. It was becoming common procedure in a blackout.

Clover flicked her screen, but nothing happened. "I'm out of power," she groaned.

"Me too!" said Cassie.

"Same here," Leona chimed in.

More shouts rang up and down the rows as everyone realized the same thing: none of their Star-Zaps were working.

Lady Cordial jumped up. "Don't panic!" she cried in a voice that sounded quite panicky. "As long as we have the s-s-s-stars, we will have light."

Just then a giant storm cloud rolled across the sky, dimming each and every star. A few raindrops fell, then more and more. The stadium was plunged into darkness.

Frightened and wet, girls rushed to the exits, pushing each other.

The Star Darlings stayed in their seats. Clover thought quickly. She knew the dangers of crowded venues: their big top tent had collapsed once, and the audience had barely gotten out in time.

"We have to do something," she told the others. "Leona! Does your mic still work?"

"Testing, one, two, three. Yes!"

"Tell everyone to return to their seats. The rain is letting up now, so that's better."

"Everyone," Leona declared into the microphone, "return to your seats!"

No one was listening. Instead, even more Starlings rushed into the aisles.

"Give them a reason," Clover ordered Leona. "And be louder."

Leona took a deep breath. "Starlings!" she said in a strong, commanding way. "Return to your seats. I will be raffling the chance to perform with the Star Darlings band by seat number." Leona spoke with such force that each Starling stopped in her tracks.

Some did turn around. But most, Clover realized with dismay, didn't seem all that interested in performing with Leona—at least when they were in the middle of a blackout. So Scarlet brought out her drumsticks to play a *rat-a-tat-tat* on the mic, and everyone stopped again.

At the same moment, Cassie opened up her bag and

lifted out something furry and glowing. *What* is *that?* Clover wondered.

"Now is as good a time as any," Cassie murmured. The creature lifted its head and Clover realized Cassie was holding a small pink glowfur. It was adorable, of course. They all were, with their big soulful eyes, delicate gossamer wings, and huggable plump bodies.

"She's yours?" Clover asked in starprise.

Leona glanced over. "Oh, my stars, is that a glowfur?" she cried.

Cassie nodded. "I've had Itty with me since the first day of school," she admitted. "I know we're not supposed to have pets. But I was so nervous coming to a big school and being with so many people I didn't know, I just had to have her close by."

Cassie paused as Itty nestled under her chin. "I brought her tonight because, well, you know how I feel, Clover. And she always makes me feel better."

Clover nodded.

"But I can't keep her a secret anymore. It wouldn't be right." Cassie held Itty close and whispered, "Sing the 'Song of Calmness.'"

Leona held out her mic, and the glowfur began to sing. Her voice was pure and tinkling, the melody soothing. The panic subsided immediately. Slowly, carefully, everyone returned to their seats as if in a trance.

"Give it all you've got," Leona instructed the glowfur, and Itty's song swelled. It grew louder and louder, and it became a call to all her glowfur friends. In starsecs, the sky filled with the brightly lit creatures, all singing the same lullaby.

A feeling of peace swept through the crowd.

"Now lead the way out," Cassie instructed, and the glowfurs flew to various sections of the stadium and guided the Starlings to the exits. The crisis was averted.

Later, swinging in her hammock when the events of the night had passed, Clover felt relieved. Everyone had gotten out safely. Astra was happy the game had ended in a tie, just before the opposing team surely would have scored. And in the commotion, no one but the Star Darlings knew where that first glowfur had come from. So Cassie's secret pet was, luckily, still a secret.

"You know," Clover told Astra, "I think we should offer to help Lady Cordial more. You had a team dinner, so you weren't at the Celestial Café tonight. But all the Bot-Bot waiters stopped working at the very same starsec. Remember Lady Cordial had sent that holo-message, explaining she'd be putting them on power-save mode to conserve energy?"

"Mmmm-hmmmm," Astra said sleepily.

"Well, it turns out that she accidentally switched them to hyperdrive instead," Clover said. "They all had to be rebooted. But everything's okay. At least for now."

She waited for Astra to say something—about Lady Cordial, about the energy crisis, about her lead-off goal. But Astra must have been running low on energy herself. She was already fast asleep.

Clover raced through dark streets. She was rushing to catch the circus swift train, not sure where she needed to go but fully aware she was awfully late. And if she missed the train? Clover's heart thudded in her chest. She'd never ever find it. Her family would be lost to her forever. She couldn't miss it. She just couldn't!

At the opposite end of the street, Clover glimpsed someone—she couldn't tell who—searching for her. "Clover?" called the figure. "Where are you?"

"I'm here!" she shouted. "I'm here!"

"I'm here!" Clover was still crying when she woke with a start. It had all been a dream!

She glanced anxiously at Astra. Luckily, her roommate, exhausted from the game, was still fast asleep. Clover reached for her Star-Zap, now working properly, and checked the time. She'd barely been asleep at all!

What an odd dream, she thought, sitting back in her hammock. She should definitely talk to Piper about it. Maybe it meant she was missing something. That she had to get to a certain destination before it was too late? And who was that Starling who'd been searching for her? Her voice was very familiar. . . .

"Clover?" called the same voice, coming from the other side of the door.

It was Piper, just outside her room!

Clover padded to the door and opened it quietly. "Piper," she whispered. "What in Starland are you doing here?"

Piper, her eyes closed, half nodded, then waved one arm languidly. *She's sleepwalking!* Clover realized. *And she wants me to follow her.*

Clover tentatively touched Piper's arm, but Piper slept on. Clover had read somewhere that you shouldn't wake a sleepwalker. So as Piper turned to go, Clover had no choice but to follow. She couldn't just let her wander around by herself.

Piper led Clover to the Big Dipper Dorm and opened

the door to a supply closet. It had to be the closet Scarlet used to go down to the caves. Clover hesitated. She really didn't like the idea of going underground with a sleep-walking Piper in the middle of the night—especially after getting trapped in a secret chamber just the other starweek.

But Piper was already inside, reaching for a trapdoor as if she knew exactly where it was. Soundlessly, she started down the steps.

Glad she was still clutching her Star-Zap, Clover set it to flashlight mode and followed. Moving quietly and quickly, the two went down the metal stairs—cool beneath Clover's bare feet—and into the underground tunnels.

The tunnels were a mazelike jumble. After a few starmins, Clover had no idea where they were. But Piper floated down the halls, sure-footed and confident, seem-ingly with a destination in mind. Then they turned left, and even in the gloom, Piper recognized the tunnel. It led to the Wish Cavern.

With a knowing nod, Piper stopped at a random spot and flicked a wrist at the wall. The hidden door whooshed open, and they stepped inside.

The Wish Cavern! Each time Clover saw it, she felt starmazed. They were deep underground, but starlight flooded the space as if they were standing in an open field. Golden waterfalls of wish energy still flowed down the cavern walls. But Clover noted the streams had narrowed and the current was sluggish. Then she turned to the center of the room, where a grassy platform stood, and she froze.

A Wish Orb was waiting.

"Piper?" she said questioningly. But before Clover could say another word, the orb floated through the air. It stopped, hovering star inches from Clover's nose. Without thinking, Clover reached for it and held it gently in her palm.

Now what? she wondered. Piper's eyes were still closed, and she was swaying on her feet as if in a trance. She'd be no help. But without Lady Stella—or Lady Cordial—to mark the occasion, there was no ceremony, no pomp, no starcumstance. Clover felt slightly disappointed. She was a circus performer, after all. She liked a bit of fanfare.

Then Piper spoke in a strange, sleepy, drawn-out voice. "The orb has been waiting for you to come, Clover. Time is running out for your Wish Mission."

Piper's voice grew more forceful. "You must leave right now!"

CHAPTER
6

Clover gasped. Leave right then? In the middle of the night? In her bare feet? Without a word to Lady Cordial?

Besides, did Piper even know what she was talking about? The Starling wasn't even awake!

It was all so unusual, and Clover didn't like it one bit. She should just go back to her hammock, pull up her blanket, and go back to sleep. Then she'd wake up, and maybe there'd be a group holo-text telling the Star Darlings a Wish Orb had been identified. There'd be the usual routine of the platform opening, the orb floating into the cavern, and the girls waiting for the orb to choose its Starling.

But right there, right then, she was already holding the Wish Orb—without the Star Darlings. Without Lady Stella. And she didn't know what to do.

Clover's Wish Orb trembled. Its sparkle dimmed. *Starf!* she thought. The orbs had notoriously short life cycles. Clover had to help grant her Wisher's wish before it faded away. And if she didn't do it in time? The energy would be lost forever. Not to mention her poor Wisher's dream would never come true.

Clover groaned in frustration. She was the eleventh Star Darling to be chosen. She'd waited so long for this to happen. (Not as long as Gemma, of course.) And now here was her opportunity, her chance to excel.

A flutterfocus darted by, and Clover gazed at it in wonder. It fluttered here and there, swooping around the platform as if searching for sweet-smelling nectar. It hovered for a moment, made up its mind, and landed lightly on Piper's nose.

Piper's eyes snapped open. She stared at the creature for a long moment, then held out her finger. The flutterfocus settled on the tip. "Hello, little one," Piper said softly. A moment later, the creature took off, disappearing behind a golden waterfall.

"Star greetings, Clover," Piper said with a calm smile. She gazed around the Wish Cavern as if it was exactly where she'd expected to be. All along, Clover had resisted the urge to shake Piper awake. Now she resisted the urge just to shake her. How could any Starling be so . . . so . . . unruffled?

"Aren't you starprised?" Clover asked a bit shrilly. "You're underground, in the Wish Cavern!"

"Of course I'm starprised," Piper replied. "But there must be a reason why I'm here—with you." She eyed the Wish Orb. Clover relaxed her grip. She'd been holding it a little too firmly.

"So tell me," Piper continued.

With a sigh, Clover explained how Piper had come to her room and led her underground. Piper nodded as if that kind of thing happened every starday.

"So what do you think I should do?" Clover's mind was racing like a runaway galliope, and at least Piper was composed and capable of clear thought.

"I already told you." Piper spoke with exaggerated patience, as if Clover was a wee Starling. "You need to go right now."

Oh! So she remembered that part! Clover thought. *How helpful!*

Clover knew Piper was right. Still, she hated to just leave! "Shouldn't we wake up Lady Cordial?"

"I don't think so," Piper said thoughtfully. "There's

no time. And I don't want to bother her. The poor Starling really needs her rest."

Clover definitely agreed with that. But there were other issues. "I don't have my hat! I'm in my pajamas!" she said.

"Your Star-Zap has a Wishworld Outfit Selector," Piper said reasonably. "And you'd have to change anyway."

"What about the Wishworld backpack? I need a place to store my shooting star!"

Piper thought for a moment. "I'll run back to the room and grab mine. We'll also need some safety star-glasses. Then we can go straight to the Wishworld Surveillance Deck."

Clover shrugged. "Okay," she said. She was out of arguments. Then she thought of something.

"My Wish Pendant!" she cried. "I can't go without that."

"It's right there, in your hair."

Clover reached for the purple barrette, decorated with three silvery stars. It was still there! Luckily, she hadn't taken it off before bed.

It was all happening so quickly. But that was the way it had to be, she supposed. The two girls left the Wish Cavern and made their way back to the dorm. Clover waited outside as Piper slipped into her room. She reappeared holding a blue backpack, the door sliding shut behind her. "Couldn't find mine," she said. "So I grabbed Vega's. I'm sure she won't mind." With a shrug, Clover grabbed the backpack and slung it over her shoulder. The two Starlings then headed to the Wishworld Surveillance Deck.

The girls kept to the shadows as they crept across campus. The Bot-Bot guards were on high alert that time of night, and the Starlings didn't want to be questioned.

They were just nearing the band shell when Clover spied a guard circling the Star Quad. She pulled Piper behind a statue of the mythical Atlight, holding up Starland. She'd always loved those stories. Her uncle Fabrizzio, the strongman at the circus, knew glowzens by heart.

Clover and Piper waited for the guard to pass. Then, breathing a sigh of relief, Clover stepped out from the safety of the statue—and bumped right into another Bot-Bot.

"Star greetings, Miss Clover and Miss Piper," said the Bot-Bot. Then he winked.

"Is that you, Mojo?" Clover asked. Mojo—MO-J4—was not your typical Bot-Bot. Sage had met him her first day at Starling Academy when he gave her family a tour. From then on, he had checked in on her now and again, and the two had developed a friendship. Sage swore the Bot-Bot had his own sweet personality. But Clover had never really talked to him—until now. And now wasn't a very good time. After all, she and Piper were roaming around campus at night, an activity that was strictly against the rules.

"Yes, it is I," Mojo answered. "I am on security detail tonight. It is a change of pace for me, and a little boring, I might add. But now I meet you two! How nice."

It was true that Mojo didn't talk like a typical Bot-Bot. But did that mean he wouldn't turn them in?

"Well, Mojo, we couldn't sleep," Clover explained, "so Piper and I are taking a walk."

"Yes," Piper added. "We're heading to the observation deck."

Clover nudged Piper warningly, trying to convey the message *Too much information! Not a good thing!*

"It is a lovely night for stargazing," Mojo said with another wink. "Please allow me to accompany you."

Clover smiled. With a Bot-Bot by their side, she and Piper wouldn't be stopped. "Star salutations, Mojo. Can we hurry? If we don't move quickly, we'll miss the . . . the meteor shower."

Mojo led the way past the band shell and Halo Hall, talking at full volume, as if it was the middle of the afternoon and the girls were going to class. When they reached the Flash Vertical Mover that would zip them up to the deck, he gave a little bow.

He turned to leave but stopped when Clover exclaimed, "Oh! The mover is turned off. Lady Cordial's orders to conserve energy, I guess."

"Please allow me to be of assistance," Mojo said. Using one of his tool-like fingers, he lifted a plate by the mover door and connected two wires. The lights flashed. The mover hummed. "There you go. I'll just wait here so I can turn it off when you're done."

What would Mojo think when Piper came down alone? "Don't worry about it, Mojo," said Clover. "Just turn it off after we reach the top. We can walk down the emergency stairs when we're ready."

Piper raised her eyebrows but said nothing. Mojo nodded and said, "As you wish."

"Of course you mean *I'll* walk down," Piper told Clover as they zoomed to the top. The mover doors slid open, and the girls stepped onto the deck.

"First things first," Clover said, trying to think of all the steps involved. "We need to put on our safety starglasses and find a star."

Piper put on her seafoam green glasses and handed Clover her pair. Clover slipped them on. It was funny to see the world through Vega's blue-tinted starglasses. While she preferred her usual purple, she did notice that she felt cool and a bit more relaxed.

Together, Clover and Piper scanned the heavens. "There's a bunch right there!" Clover pointed to a cluster of stars moving quickly across the sky.

The girls grabbed the wrangler ropes—strands of positive energy braided into lassos. They kept their eyes on the shooting stars. "That one is coming closer . . . closer . . . closer . . ." Clover shouted. "Now throw!"

They flung their ropes into space. Both fell woefully short.

"Another one is coming. Let's try throwing them like Frisbeams," Clover suggested.

"Okay," said Piper, planting her feet and changing her grip.

"Now go!" Clover cried. Piper let go, and her rope whooshed through the air—and settled over Clover. "Well, you did rope a star. A circus star," Clover joked. "But why don't you just watch me this time?"

Clover flicked her wrist—hard—and her rope sailed into space, falling neatly around a star. "Yes!" said Clover.

She tried to pull it in, but the star bucked and lurched like a wild galliope. "Help me, Piper!"

Piper reached to grab hold of the rope just above Clover's hands. They both held on tight. But the star jerked even harder.

"We're losing it!" said Clover breathlessly. Piper was not much help.

"I'm doing the best I can," Piper said calmly. She was panting and her knuckles had turned lightning white. Clover knew she really was trying. But how would they ever do this? She'd never realized how strong a Star Wrangler had to be. The most she and Piper could manage was keeping the star in place.

"Greetings again!" said a familiar voice. "I thought I'd observe the meteor shower, too. But this looks like much more fun. May I join in?"

Wrangling a star was definitely against student rules! But Mojo was already over the half wall, zipping into the inky blackness and tugging at the rope. Working together, all three towed the star to the edge of the deck, Clover and Piper stepping back farther with every tug.

Finally, the star hovered by the wall. It was ready to go. But was Clover?

"Now what?" asked Mojo.

"We strap Clover in," Piper answered.

By then Clover had stopped worrying about Mojo's reaction. She was just happy he was there.

Piper and Mojo quickly got Clover's legs in place, fastening the safety buckles tightly. But the waist belt wouldn't click into place. The whole thing was like a circus, Clover thought. A comedy routine the clowns would perform.

Even worse, there was no adult in charge, no one to give advice and reassure her or make her believe in herself. She missed Lady Stella.

Finally, Piper realized the buckle was upside down, and she fumbled the latch into place. "There," she said, satisfied. "Ready to go?"

"No!" The star was already pulling Clover over the balcony. But she hung on to the wall tightly, trying to stay a bit longer. She needed to feel this was an official mission. She needed to follow the regular routine.

"Let me practice my Mirror Mantra first."

"Sure," said Piper as Mojo struggled to keep hold. "What is it?"

"Keep the beat and shine like the star you are." Once she said it out loud, Clover felt better. Still, she needed a few parting words of wisdom.

"Piper, can you wish me well? Say something wise? I need some closure before I go!"

"Of course, of course," Piper said soothingly. She thought a moment. Meanwhile, Mojo almost lost his grip.

As she closed her eyes, Mojo's grip loosened even more. "Clover, may you always remember to—oh, *starf*!" Piper finished as the lasso slipped out of Mojo's hands.

"Gooooood-bye!" Clover called as she rocketed away. That was not the way she wanted to go!

But just as Starland slipped out of sight, she heard a voice, speaking from close by, perhaps inside her very own head.

"Sometimes the simplest solution is the most powerful one."

It sounded like the headmistress. Not Lady Cordial—Lady Stella. The true head of the school, Clover still believed in her heart of hearts.

"Lady Stella?" she said aloud.

She held her breath, hoping for an answer.

Finally, she sighed. Of course Lady Stella—wherever she was—had no idea Clover had just taken off on a Wish Mission. And maybe no one had said those words at all; she was just being silly and sentimental.

Sometimes the simplest solution is the most powerful one, she repeated to herself. Then she pushed those words out of her mind. She still had to choose an outfit, change, ready herself for the mission, and, of course, take in the sights. All those streaming lights and planets! It really was starmazing.

In no time at all, Clover's Star-Zap signaled her to prepare for landing. Her journey was just about over.

"Wishworld, here I come!"

CHAPTER
7

"Ouch!" Clover landed on a hard surface, jarring her bare feet. She'd already changed into Wishworld clothes—a sparkly purple miniskirt and fringed jacket. Of course she'd chosen a hat, too—a cute purple cap with a brim that covered her face. But she hadn't been wearing shoes before, so she'd forgotten to pick a new pair.

Quickly, Clover scrolled through some choices and settled on a pair of purple flats. Instantly, they were on her feet. She took a tentative step and smiled. The landing hadn't been so rough after all; already her feet felt fine.

Before she did anything else, Clover picked up her shooting star, folded it up, and placed it carefully in the front pocket of her backpack.

That accomplished, Clover gazed around, trying to get her bearings. She seemed to be in some sort of open-air building. Parallel yellow lines were painted on the cement floor in neat rows.

Finally, she saw a sign: G2. That was a funny name for a building. But then again, maybe all Wishling buildings were called by letters and numbers and no other Star Darling had noticed it. She wondered if she should add it to her Cyber Journal. Then she decided against it. She wasn't sure, and anyway, right then she needed to get going. She most likely wouldn't even have time for observations on her mission, since she had gotten such a late start.

First step: find her Wisher.

Clover flicked her Star-Zap for directions. She followed the route, going around and around the building, walking down ramps separating floors marked F, E, D, C, B, and then A. *Hmmm, the letters must be for levels,* she thought, glad she hadn't entered the observation in the journal. That would have been slightly embarrassing.

Also, she noted the lined spaces were for Wishling vehicles. She recognized them from looking through the Starland telescope. But they seemed much more primitive up close, with clunky shapes and actual wheels. As

Clover went lower and lower, more and more spaces were filled.

Beep! A vehicle was coming right at her, honking like a glowgoose! Clover jumped out of the way just in time. *These Wishlings should slow down,* she thought, moving to the side, where she thought it would be safer.

She checked the directions again and found a door marked PARKING GARAGE EXIT. That's where she was! A parking garage. A sign below it read MALL ENTRANCE.

Mall, she said to herself. It sounded familiar. She'd learned about it in Wishling Ways . . . something about a place where teenagers "hung out" and shopped for friends. Basically, that was what she'd be doing. Making friends with your Wisher was the first step to finding out the wish. So the location seemed promising!

Stepping inside the mall, Clover was immediately surrounded by people. There were some teenagers. But the crowd was really a mix of all ages: some adults pushing little wheeled vehicles with wee Wishlings inside, Wishling kids holding their parents' hands, older Wishlings walking in pairs. They all held bags and rushed here and there with determined looks on their faces.

She peered around the Wishlings and realized store after store lined the walls. Clothing stores, shoe stores, toy stores, many with signs that read BACK TO SCHOOL SALE! *So this must be the end of the Wishling warm weather break,* Clover thought. And teenagers didn't shop *for* friends there; they shopped *with* them! Along with everyone else.

A mall was really just a star-shopping center—only not half as stellar. Yes, there were moving steps in the middle, but it was nothing like the Cosmic Transporter. Plus there was no Choose-Your-Sparkle Shop or Groom-Your-Glowfur Corner. Not quite as useful a place—she'd have to tell the other Star Darlings.

Still, it was interesting. The mall was one long rectangle. It had an open center space with moving steps taking people from level to level and a very nice glass roof that let in the afternoon sun.

Clover leaned over a railing so the rays hit her face, then she moved on. *Wait!* Were those carts in the middle of the floor? Vehicles with wheels? She jumped out of the way, expecting them to come at her like the car in the garage. Then she realized the carts weren't actually moving. They were really mini-stores that specialized in very odd items.

One, with a sign reading HEADCASES, had only strange little statues with giant heads that bobbed when you touched them. Another sold miniature scenes in clear rounded plastic containers. She shook one that showed Wishlings wearing heavy coats, scarves, and hats, and tiny snowflakes fell on their heads. That made sense. But when she shook a beach scene, snow fell, too!

Suddenly, Clover noticed something familiar: Starland-like creatures!

Creatures that resembled glions and galliopes were grouped in a circle, just waiting to be petted. Clover rushed over, looking for starapples or some other snack to feed them. But when she got closer, she discovered they weren't real. In fact, they were part of a ride. Kids clambered on top of the fake creatures, which then moved around and around on a platform to sprightly music. Interesting.

Next Clover wandered into a hat store just for fun. She caught sight of her plain Wishworld self in a mirror. Even though she'd been expecting to see dull skin and Wishling-colored hair, it was still a bit of a starprise. Of course, she felt glad she could pass for any old mall visitor. And she did have a bright purple streak left in her hair, an occurrence many Star Darlings had already mentioned. So it could have been worse.

"Oh!" Clover cried as she spied a floppy purple hat. Maybe she could wear that instead of the cap! She plunked it on her head and checked out her reflection. It did look good. But then a sales Wishling walked over and asked, "Would you like to see more in that style?"

"No, ah, ah, thank you!" Clover said, hurrying out. How could she forget she had no Wishworld currency?

Not only that, but she'd been wasting valuable time shopping! *You're already way behind schedule,* Clover scolded herself. *Now get moving!*

Not even glancing at any other shop windows, concentrating only on her directions, Clover went up two levels and found herself following signs to the "Food Court."

Another oddity, thought Clover. Hadn't she learned that Wishlings played sports on courts, too? Did they eat meals surrounded by balls and nets and whatever other equipment they used? No, she realized as she stepped into the bustling space. There were only tables and small takeout restaurants. Most had food words in their names: Bongo Burger; Pizza, Pizza, Pizza; and The Smoothie Shack. Clover felt proud that she recognized most of the Wishling food names. But wait—there was one called The Sushi Spot. On Starland, Sushi was the most popular singer on the planet! Wait until she told Leona!

Again, Clover glanced at her directions. They ended there, at the entrance to the food court. So her Wisher must be at one of the tables or waiting in line. How could she possibly find her in this crowded place?

She took a few steps, moving closer to The Sushi Spot for lack of a better plan. Suddenly, she felt a slight vibration on her head. The Wish Pendant barrette! Good thing the cap was covering it. Otherwise, everyone would notice its glow.

Clover wove through the tables haphazardly at first, changing directions on the strength of the Wish Pendant's vibration. As she neared one table with a daughter and mother, the barrette pulsed so strongly that Clover stopped suddenly. The Wishling girl, staring with narrowed eyes at her mom, must be Clover's Wisher.

A couple was just leaving the next table, so Clover slipped into an empty chair. Immediately, her nose wrinkled in distaste. The Wishlings hadn't cleared their trays, which were covered with crumpled napkins and leftover food! And unlike on Starland, the mess would stay right there unless someone cleared it away. *That most certainly won't be me!* Clover thought.

She turned to her Wisher just as the girl, upset over something her mother had said, tossed her head. Clover grinned happily. The girl had a purplish streak in her hair—not quite as bright and shiny as Clover's, but it was a streak nonetheless, standing out in her long blond hair. They had something in common!

"I am not happy with you, Ruby Marshall," the mom was saying. "How could you go and dye your hair like that without asking permission? And purple of all colors. It looks ridiculous!"

Humph, thought Clover, a little insulted. Of course, it was different there. She knew that Wishlings had to add chemicals to their hair to make it look Starland-normal. *How sad for them*, Clover thought. And apparently, the procedure was frowned upon by adult Wishlings—at least when their children were involved.

"Stop it, Mom," the girl answered. "You are so old-fashioned. No one thinks a purple streak is a big deal anymore. Look around! Lots of kids do it!"

Clover took off her cap, expecting the mom to do what her daughter asked—look around. Once she spotted Clover, she'd realize her daughter was right.

But the mom just shook her head, glaring at the girl. The girl glared back, not noticing Clover's hair, either.

This was Clover's big chance to meet her Wisher. She needed to act quickly. She had to get the girl's attention so she'd see Clover's streak, realize they had lots in common, and want to be her friend.

Reining in her repulsion, Clover picked up the heavy food trays and carried them to the garbage container right next to the Wishlings. She made a big show of pushing against the swinging door to empty the tray.

The girl looked up. "Hey!" she called out. "I like your hair! See, Mom? I told you purple hair is not a big deal at all!"

Clover smiled at the mom. The mom frowned back.

"Did you use Splatter?" the girl asked excitedly. She held up a long lock of her streaked hair and examined it closely. "Yours is better," she said decidedly. "I definitely missed a few spots."

"You have to leave it on longer than the directions say," Clover said, as if she knew what she was talking about.

"Did your mom get mad when you did it?" the girl asked eagerly.

Her mom finally gazed up, meeting Clover's eyes. She didn't look angry now, just sad. She had a kind, open face—very similar to the girl's—with big brown eyes.

Clover shrugged, trying to be noncommittal.

"No, really. Is she angry about your purple hair?" the girl insisted.

"No," Clover said truthfully, stopping short of

saying her mother was actually thrilled. She and her mom had the same shade.

"See, Mom? I'm the only one who gets treated like a baby!"

The girl stared at Clover, taking in her outfit with approval. "And are you allowed to pick out your own clothes?"

"Yes, I am."

"I'm not," the girl said quickly, giving her mom a significant look. "My mother chooses all my clothes. Like I said, she treats me like a baby."

At this, the mom finally spoke. "Ruby Marshall! I only want you to wear clothes that are appropriate! You know I hate leggings and short tops that don't adequately cover your posterior!" She looked at her watch and stood up. "It's almost time for your appointment. I'm heading to the ladies' room and I'll be back in a minute."

With her mom gone, the girl deflated slightly. "My purple streaks are history. My mom's taking me to Snippy's to dye it back." She sighed loudly. "I wish she'd let me grow up!"

Clover felt a tingle run down her spine and her mouth fell open in starprise. She'd barely said two words to the girl, but she'd already discovered her wish. How easy could a mission be? *Thank the stars*, she thought, since time was of the essence!

Clover sat in the mom's seat and smiled. "I know I'm lucky. My parents talk to me like a . . . a person! Not a wee Star—I mean, little kid."

Clover couldn't even imagine her mom babying her. She'd always been treated like an important member of the circus family, with jobs and responsibilities. Even before she could walk, she had been crawling around to retrieve ozziefruit for juggling acts and sitting on top of spinning chairs. Once she could talk, she offered opinions about starwire performances. Poor Ruby Marshall. She really needed Clover's help.

"My name is Clover," she said in a friendly way.

"I'm Ruby."

Ruby slid her tray toward Clover. "Here, want some french fries?"

Clover realized she was hungry. She followed Ruby's lead and dipped the long objects into some red sauce. A smile spread across her face. They were delicious! Before she knew it, she had finished them all.

"Sorry," she said.

"No problem," said Ruby. "I'm kind of too nervous to eat, anyway."

"How come?" asked Clover.

"School is starting soon," said Ruby, clearly embarrassed.

"Where do you go to school?" Clover asked, knowing exactly what she'd say when Ruby answered.

"Westlake Prep." Ruby's eyes flashed—with excitement or nervousness, Clover couldn't tell. "It'll be my first year."

"Me too!" Clover said quickly. "I'll be a first year at Westlake, too!"

"That's so sick," said Ruby excitedly.

Clover frowned for a moment, then remembered that the word had two meanings, at least to young Wishlings.

"Yeah, sick!" she replied, feeling slightly silly.

"It's going to be so different," Ruby went on. "The school is really big and there'll be so many people I don't know! It would have been nice to have an older brother or sister who was going there, too, to show me around."

In Clover's circus family, there was always someone older to help you with a new act and always someone younger who needed your help. "Well, at least you can do that for your younger siblings," she suggested.

Ruby shook her head. "Uh-uh. I'm an only child. I

loved it when I was little. I had my parents' total attention. But now it's too much attention! My mom watches over me like a hawk."

Clover didn't know what a hawk was. But she guessed it was some sort of security system.

"I'm back," Ruby's mom—Mrs. Marshall—announced. "Time to go."

"M-o-o-o-o-m," Ruby said, stretching out the word. "Clover and I are starting Westlake together. We have to talk!"

"Well, I'm sorry, girls." And Ruby's mom did look sorry, Clover thought. "Why don't you make plans to get together before school starts?"

That was nice of Mrs. Marshall, given that she didn't approve of Clover's hair, and possibly Clover herself.

"Yes!" said Ruby. "Hey, want to shop for school supplies together? We can meet right here tomorrow. I'll bring the list."

Supplies for school? On Starland, students didn't really have supplies. They used their Star-Zaps for just about everything. Of course, here students had cell phones, which could only handle a bare minimum of tasks but still served Wishlings in a similar way. "What do we need besides our phones?" Clover asked.

"I know, right?" said Ruby. She laughed, as if Clover was being funny on purpose. Ruby insisted on exchanging numbers, just in case—so Clover input Ruby's number and called her, not entirely sure it would ring. Luckily, it did. But they promised to meet in the same spot first thing in the morning.

"Come on, Ruby!" Mrs. Marshall called, already outside the food court.

Clover waved good-bye. What should she do next? She had to fill the time between then and the following morning. She looked longingly at her backpack, where the invisible tent—complete with comfy bed—was just waiting to be used. Then she looked at her Countdown Clock. So much time had passed! Did she even have time for rest?

Yes, she decided. Realistically, she couldn't do any wish granting until she saw Ruby in the morning. She couldn't follow her now. Ruby would think she was weird. And what would her mom say? She'd tell Ruby she couldn't hang out with the strange stalking girl. Clover had to stay on everyone's good side for her mission to work!

That settled it. She was going to find an empty space somewhere, set up her tent, rest, and use the time to come up with a plan to help Ruby. The top floor of the parking garage would be a good empty place, she decided.

She hurried through the mall, retracing her steps to the garage: out the exit, up the ramps, straight to the top.

"Ugh," she groaned. That level was filled, too, and drivers were circling, looking for spots, zipping quickly up and down rows, tires screeching around turns. She certainly couldn't set up an invisible tent there. Wishling drivers were crazy! It wouldn't do at all.

But she didn't want to go far. Maybe she could find an out-of-the-way place where cars weren't allowed. She searched around corners and found a large empty space with a sign that read NO PARKING. EMERGENCY USE ONLY.

Well, this will do, Clover thought. As far as she was concerned, she was in an emergency situation. She walked to the far end of the spot, leaned against the wall, and unzipped the main compartment of her backpack.

It was empty.

CHAPTER
8

"**What? There's no tent** in the backpack?" Clover searched through the side pockets and the big front one, where she'd packed the shooting star. They were all empty, too, aside from the star. She turned the backpack upside down and shook it. Nothing. Had Vega forgotten her invisible tent on Wishworld, or were they one-time use only? In any event, it didn't matter. Clover was out of luck.

Why, oh, why hadn't she used mind control on Ruby's mom when she'd had the chance? She could be staying in a cozy, warm house, not in a drafty garage without a tent!

So what next? If she hurried to the hair salon . . . What was it called? Flippy's? Tippy's? Snippy's! That was it! If she left right away, she could still catch Ruby and her mom.

But the mall was big. Very big. Clover made several wrong turns before she discovered that the mall had a map. Finally, she located Snippy's, full of salon chairs and mirrors, and walked inside.

Someone was sweeping hair from the floor. *Yuck!* Another worker was talking into a device that looked a bit like a cell phone but had a cord that plugged into the wall. Stylists were snipping, washing, drying, and brushing their customers' hair. Clover peered around. She could only see the customers' backs. But one had long, straight blond hair. *Ruby!*

"Excuse me," she said, using the correct phrase, as she stepped between Ruby and the facing mirror. Only, when she was face to face with the blonde, she realized that it wasn't Ruby. It was a woman she'd never seen before—with big thick glasses and a wide round face, her mouth falling open in surprise.

Clover did the first thing that crossed her mind. "Here, I think you dropped something," she said. But when she bent down, the only thing she found was a long lock of blond hair. She handed it to the confused woman. Then she raced outside.

She kept running until she saw an empty bench,

where she sat down to think. Okay, she'd missed Ruby. So she could forget about staying with her. The night stretched in front of Clover, and she had nowhere to go and nothing to do. *What time does the mall close, anyway?* she wondered.

Just then a young woman walked over and handed Clover a flyer. She marveled at the feel of the paper, about to crumple it into a ball, just for fun. But a big word on top caught her attention: FREE!

Clover read on.

FOCUS GROUP: FREE MOVIE SCREENING! BE THE FIRST TO SEE THE NOT-YET-RELEASED FILM VAMPIRE'S KISS. FILL OUT SHORT QUESTIONNAIRE AFTERWARDS. FREE SNACKS PROVIDED!

Clover checked a big clock on the mall wall and realized the movie would be starting shortly. *Perfect*, she thought.

By then it was getting late, and the crowds were thinning. Clover found the movie theater, handed in her flyer, and walked into the lobby. A good number of people were already there. They were all Wishlings around Clover's age. *Too bad Ruby isn't here*, she thought.

She went to the concession center and decided on white fluffy food called popcorn, crispy chips with yellow sauce called nachos, and some root beer, whatever that was. Clover hurried into the theater, carefully balancing her treats. She settled into a seat in the back row. The snacks were good, she thought. But she wasn't so sure about the movie. A strangely pale teenage boy with two sharp teeth kept chasing people.

Was it supposed to be scary? Funny? Clover couldn't tell. She was more interested in the lack of technology. There was an actual screen, onto which flat moving pictures were projected. She thought how different it was from home, where everything seemed so real and solid, floating in the air right in front of your eyes.

After the film ended, she filled out the questionnaire as best she could. People around her had seemed to enjoy the movie, so she held back her own opinions. Maybe she couldn't be the best critic, coming from another world and all.

She wandered around the mall, thinking about a plan to help Ruby and wondering what to do next. And there, right in front of her, like a dream come true, was a furniture store with a bedroom display in the window. The bed looked so inviting and comfy that Clover wanted to crawl under the covers and close her eyes. And she could, she realized, with the help of a little mind control.

Quickly, Clover stepped inside.

"I'm sorry," said a woman with a name tag that read LINDA. "We're closing up."

"That's okay," Clover told Linda. "I'm going to stay overnight . . . as part of a focus group . . . to test the bed in the window." She looked deeply into the woman's eyes.

"You're going to stay overnight to test the bed," Linda repeated as if in a trance, "as part of a focus group." Then, in a more normal voice, she added, "I think I'll stop off at the bakery and pick up some chocolate croissants. For some reason, I feel like I can smell them right now!"

Clover grinned. It was hard to believe that adult Wishlings would do what you said just because you made them smell favorite treats from their childhoods. But clearly, it really did happen!

"I'll turn off the lights," Clover said.

"You'll turn off the lights," Linda said. Then she left, locking up behind her.

Alone in the store, Clover walked through displays of dining rooms, living rooms, and bedrooms. She stopped in front of a full-length mirror to say her Mirror Mantra to herself: "Keep the beat and shine like the star you are."

Immediately, her reflection began to sparkle and she felt more focused, ready to refine the plan she'd come up with earlier.

The goal: to get Ruby's parents to see she was a young adult so they would stop treating her like a baby.

The strategy: to help Ruby prove herself and show her parents she was mature and responsible. Being responsible herself, Clover knew exactly what was involved. And she believed that helping Ruby prove herself was surely the way to go. She was still a little fuzzy, though, on how to do it. Suddenly, her eyes fell on a picture frame for sale. It held a generic family photo—two parents, three young children.

That was it! Ruby could babysit. She would earn money, and then she could open her own bank account. Not only would she prove she was capable and steady, but she'd have money to buy her own clothes.

The plan was complete! *Now*, Clover thought, *I can rest.* She changed into a comfortable pair of violet pajamas with the help of her Wishworld Outfit Selector and slipped between the sheets of the comfy bed in the window. Within minutes, she fell fast asleep.

★

Clover slept soundly. Hours passed, and she stirred a bit, her eyes still closed. Then she stiffened. For some reason, she felt like someone was watching her.

"Astra?" she murmured. Then she remembered: She was on Wishworld. In a bed. In a store window. *Starf!*

Clover opened one eye. A crowd of people stood in front of the store, pointing at her. Linda was pushing past them, opening the gates by the door. "Here is the first tester from our focus group," Linda announced. "Let's see if she's satisfied!"

Clover hopped up, hurriedly straightening the blanket. She stood in front of the crowd in her pajamas, feeling slightly silly.

"I love the bed!" she said loudly as the crowd surged into the store. "You saw for yourselves! I slept better last night than I have in starweeks . . . I mean, *weeks*!" She smiled widely.

Linda beamed.

"I was watching that girl for over half an hour," one woman said. "She absolutely slept like a baby. I want to try it out."

"Me too!" called a man.

People pressed closer to Linda, eager to put their names on a list. Clover slipped away from the crowd with a final smile and a wave and ducked into the restroom.

She emerged in a new Wishling outfit of purple leggings, an oversized black off-the-shoulder sweater, and purple-fringed ankle boots. A black fedora completed the outfit. She stole a glance in a full-length mirror in a bedroom display. Perfect. Looking at the Wishworld clock on her Star-Zap, she hurried to the food court.

Ruby was already sitting at a table, her long hair entirely blond—not a bit of purple left. It was really too bad, Clover thought. But Ruby was smiling, happy to see her.

"I got us some muffins!" Ruby said.

The muffins tasted similar to astromuffins, and Clover had two. While Ruby chatted about her friends—which ones were going to Westlake, which ones to Eastlake—Clover checked her Countdown Clock. She gulped. It was really, *really* getting late. In order to succeed, she'd have to do everything in record time.

She only hoped it was possible.

CHAPTER
9

After breakfast, the girls headed to Take Note, which was the "dopest place to buy school supplies," according to Ruby.

"Not the sickest?" Clover asked.

Ruby nodded. "That too," she said.

Clover grinned. She couldn't wait to tell her fellow Star Darlings she'd picked up a new Wishling word!

At Take Note, Clover gazed around in astonishment. *Paper!* There were notebooks, pads, stationery, envelopes, and stacks of paper everywhere. *Unbelievable!*

And what about those things called binders? How did Wishling students fit them into their backpacks? They were so large and bulky. Everything in the store was strange and fascinating—especially those writing sticks called highlighters that, disappointingly, didn't even light up.

She and Ruby loaded up their carts, and Ruby declared they were done.

Mrs. Marshall met them by the checkout, where employees stood behind clunky machines and customers passed them small plastic cards to pay with. The line snaked almost to the back of the store. While they waited, Ruby's mom reminisced about her first day of high school—back before students used what she referred to as "laptops." Ruby rolled her eyes, but Clover noticed she was actually listening.

Finally, they were next. Clover, who had no Wishling money, had a plan. She faked receiving a text. "Look at that!" she said. "Good old Mom. She already bought all my supplies for me!" She turned to Ruby. "Now I don't have to carry them home. That's ill of her."

Ruby gave her a funny look. "I think you mean 'sick.'"

"Of course," said Clover. "Totally dumb."

"Dope," corrected Ruby's mother. She laughed. "Guess I've been paying attention!"

Mother and daughter checked out while Clover put

all her school supplies back. She wished she could have kept the pack of loose-leaf, with its straight lines and perfectly placed holes. Or the purple composition note-book. That was hard to return to the rack.

"Mom," said Ruby as they left the store, "can you take my stuff home so Clover and I can hang out a little here?"

Ruby's mom paused. "I don't think so," she said. "I have to get back and I don't want you to walk home alone. I'll just drive you back."

Clover got into the backseat, and Ruby slid next to her. "My mom won't let me sit up front," she explained. "Still! My cousins are allowed to and they're younger than me! I bet even the ones in preschool will beat me to the front!"

During the drive, Clover shared her idea with Ruby, whispering so Mrs. Marshall wouldn't hear: *babysitting, money, bank account.*

"Sounds good!" Ruby agreed happily, speaking in a low voice. "My neighbor Mrs. Howard has little twin girls. They're adorable! And she just told my mom that her babysitter moved away and she's looking for a new one."

"Sounds perfect!" said Clover.

Mrs. Marshall dropped them off in front of Ruby's

house, then went to run more errands. "At least she leaves me home alone," Ruby grumbled. "Finally!"

"Let's go talk to your neighbor now," Clover suggested, glancing worriedly at her Countdown Clock. "You can line up a babysitting job and then we can tell your mother your plan." Ruby agreed.

Mrs. Howard was in her backyard. She was holding a hose as two little girls in bathing suits ran around in the spray. They were about three Wishworld years old, Clover guessed, with short curly hair and little round bellies. They weren't identical, but they looked very much alike.

Ruby waved to Mrs. Howard. "Won't be too many more summer days!" the woman said as Ruby and Clover walked closer. "I want to get them outside as much as possible."

"Oh, sure!" said Ruby. She introduced Clover, then explained that they were available for babysitting.

"Great!" Mrs. Howard said, putting down the hose. "If you're free right now, I could really use the help. I need to go to the grocery store, and it's so much easier without the girls."

Clover looked at the wee Wishlings. The girls were little angels, really, playing together nicely and amusing themselves. The babysitting job would be a snap.

Moments later, Mrs. Howard left, while the girls—
Joelle and Michaela—waved good-bye cheerfully. The
first hour was a breeze. Ruby and the girls played games
with funny names, like Red Rover, Freeze Tag, and Kick
the Can. The girls then decided to run through the
sprinkler, so Ruby turned it back on. The twins laughed
and shouted with glee. One of the girls busied herself
next to the sprinkler. Then Joelle stood up with the hose
in her hand. "Let's play!" she cried.

The next thing Clover knew, the nozzle, which must
have been loose, fell off. The hose began to snake and
buck like Clover's shooting star. The little girl was having trouble holding on to it.

"My turn!" shouted Michaela, grabbing the hose,
too. They both spun around as the hose twisted and
turned, soaking first Ruby, then Clover, then spraying
a stream of water right into the house through an open
window.

The girls fell to the ground and rolled over each
other, crushing a neat row of flowers and coating themselves in a thick layer of mud. The hose slipped out of
their hands and continued to spray the yard.

Joelle and Michaela burst into tears. The yard was a
muddy mess. So were they.

Clover and Ruby stood frozen in place, looks of

panic on their faces. It had all happened so quickly they hadn't even had time to move. And now Clover didn't have the starriest idea what to do. Her littlest relatives would be thrilled to have a muddy playground, and a little water never fazed them. They'd be laughing, not crying.

Suddenly, Ruby went into action. She raced to the side of the house and turned off the faucet. The hose slowed to a dribble, then stopped.

She scooped up both muddy girls, then held them tight and murmured comforting words. "There, there. It's all right. You're okay. It's fine."

The girls quieted, sniffled a bit, then stopped crying altogether when Ruby tickled them.

"Okay," Ruby said cheerfully, setting them on the ground. "Let's see what we can do to clean up around here!"

"Don't want to clean up!" Joelle opened her mouth to cry again.

But Ruby said quickly, "Did I say 'clean up'? I meant, what can we do to have fun around here? I say let's turn on the hose again—on low!—and watch all that mud disappear from your bodies."

She waved at Clover to twist the faucet and held the hose carefully away from the twins as she splashed water on them. They laughed hysterically. Then she moved the lawn furniture around so the muddy spaces would be in direct sunlight. "That should dry pretty fast," she said.

Next Ruby led Michaela and Joelle to the garden area, gave them shovels, and showed them how to pat down the mud and dirt while she replanted the flowers.

Clover edged over to Ruby and whispered, "What about all the water that went inside?"

Ruby nodded. "Now!" she said, standing up. "Let's check out your house and see what we can do there!"

Everyone wiped their feet on the doormat. Then they stepped through the door and into the living room. *It doesn't look good*, Clover thought.

Toys had been knocked over by the blast. Water still dripped from the open window, and there were puddles of water on the wood floor. The place was a disaster. Clover didn't even know where to begin, and meanwhile, the girls were racing around, making even more of a mess.

Ruby found some small towels in the linen closet and showed the twins how to "house skate" by placing their tiny feet on the towels and sliding around, mopping up the wet floor. They thought it was great fun.

Meanwhile, Clover dried and organized the scattered toys.

"Now what, Ruby?" asked Michaela as she handed Ruby her towel. "We skate in the kitchen? Wash that floor?"

"The girls want to clean?" Mrs. Howard said, walking in at that moment. "Ruby, you're incredible!"

"Ruby is a real *gem*!" Clover giggled, remembering Wishworld jewels, but she meant it, too. Her Wisher had taken charge, and clearly the little girls loved her.

Mrs. Howard paid Ruby with paper money, thanking her again while the twins begged her to come back and play. Smiling, Ruby and Clover left through the back door. They paused for a moment, admiring the good-as-new backyard.

"Now," Clover said, switching gears for the next step of her wish-granting plan, "we just find a bank, hurry over, and set up an account for you."

"Slow down!" Ruby laughed. "The nearest bank is about three miles away. And we can't just walk in and open an account!"

"You can't?" Clover asked. Ruby pulled up some information on her phone and showed it to Clover. "Oh, no," Clover groaned. "You need to be accompanied by a parent, with proof of address, plus identification.

"Can we manage all this?" she asked Ruby.

"Well, my mom could go with us," said Ruby. "But

we'd have to ask. And if we really need ID, I'd have to wait until school starts. They hand them out on the first day."

"When is the first day again?" Clover asked.

"Thursday."

That meant next to nothing to Clover. "Um, how many days from today?" Maybe if it was the next day, they could work things out.

"Today's Monday, so in three days."

Clover sighed. That was way too late. Her plan was too complicated. It would take too long to complete, she realized. Why did she always do that? Just like the circus idea and the trip to Mount Glint—she made everything too involved. She wanted so much to succeed, to prove herself! And she thought the more complicated the plan, the better and smarter it was.

Then Clover remembered the words she'd heard at the beginning of her journey to Wishworld: *Sometimes the simplest solution is the most powerful one.* She hadn't been thinking simply. But maybe she could now.

Simplify! Clover told herself. *Simplify.*

Just then Ruby's phone rang. She looked at the screen and then quickly put it away. "It's just my mom," she said.

"Ruby! Answer it!" said Clover. "Talk to her!"

Reluctantly, Ruby swiped the screen. "Hi, Mom."

Mrs. Marshall's voice came through the speaker loud and clear. "Where are you?" she said in a panic. "You're supposed to be at home!"

"Mom! Calm down! I'm just next door. I was baby-sitting Michaela and Joelle."

"What? Why didn't you ask permission? Why didn't you—"

"Mom! I'm hanging up. I'll be right home."

Ruby hung up and didn't move. Her mouth turned down in a pout. "I can't believe she doesn't trust me when here I am babysitting, earning my own money. She doesn't get it!"

Across the yard, Clover could see Mrs. Marshall peering anxiously from her back door.

This is definitely not helping! Clover thought. *Ruby is proving she's the opposite of mature and responsible. She should have told Ruby to ask her mom about the babysitting. And Ruby should have asked her about the hair color, too, before she dyed it. She didn't talk to her. So of course her mom got angry.*

Now she'd never get her wish—unless Clover could come up with another idea. Something simple and—

Ruby interrupted her thoughts, saying, "Let's go to

my room. I'll show you the outfit I want to wear on the first day of school. Of course, I'll have to show it to you online, because my mom won't buy it for me."

"Okay." Clover wouldn't give up! She'd stay on Wishworld with Ruby until the very last starsec.

Together, the girls went into Ruby's house. Mrs. Marshall was nowhere to be seen. But the door to the master bedroom was closed tight.

Ruby opened her door and walked inside, but Clover stood in the doorway in shock. Ruby's bedroom looked like a starclone had blown right through it.

Clothes littered the floor like a second carpet. Every surface was covered with papers. Clover could barely see the desk, dresser, or nightstand. Drawers hung half-open, with more clothes falling out of them. A jumble of shoes, blankets, and coats spilled out of the closet. The garbage can overflowed onto the rug. Dirty dishes were piled on the desk.

Clover couldn't even bring herself to walk into the room. Maybe she would just wait outside.

"Come in! Come in!" said Ruby. "Make yourself at home."

Gingerly, Clover took a step forward. She edged closer to the window, over to a teeny tiny clear space.

Peering outside, she saw a girl with bright orange hair walking down the street.

Could that be Gemma, here to help? Clover thought excitedly. She hoped against hope it was the Star Darling. She desperately needed her.

The girl drew closer, and Clover realized it was just an ordinary Wishling, not a transformed Starling. But now that she thought about it, she realized her Star Darling helper should be there any starsec. Her mission was definitely in trouble. Clover couldn't pull herself away from the window, just in case she spotted a Starling.

What was happening on Starland, anyway? Surely Piper must have told Lady Cordial about the mission. And Lady Cordial must know that it was going terribly wrong and reinforcements were needed. Then Clover's heart sank with a realization. Maybe Lady Cordial didn't know what was going on because of the lack of energy. Maybe Clover had to figure it out all by herself.

Clover slumped and yawned. Quickly, she recited her Mirror Mantra in her head—*Keep the beat and shine like the star you are*—twice. Even without a mirror, she felt a bit better. She was just about to think it a third time when Mrs. Marshall came to the door.

"Ruby Marshall," she said in a firm voice, "we really

need to talk. You need to tell me where you're going. Do you know how worried I was when I came home and you weren't here? It's important that I know your plans, in case of an emergency."

Then she turned to Clover. "You'll have to leave now, Clover. Ruby is grounded. She can't have friends over."

This was getting worse and worse. What was she going to do?

She turned and looked into the woman's eyes. "I can still stay here. It's okay."

"You can still stay here," Mrs. Marshall repeated in a dull voice. "It's okay." Then she sniffed the air. "Does anyone else smell chocolate fudge cookies?" she asked, then left before Clover or Ruby could answer.

"Wow," said Ruby. "That was weird."

"It doesn't matter," Clover told her. "And you know, don't you, that your mom is kind of right? She just worries about you, that's all. And she wants you to talk to her. Maybe if you did, she'd be more open to hearing about your ideas about your hair and clothes."

Ruby looked at her thoughtfully, considering. Giving Ruby time to think, Clover pushed aside some books and sat on the edge of the bed. She hadn't even had a starsec to come up with a new—*simple*—plan. How much time did she have left?

She opened her Countdown Clock. *Starf!* She was down to fifteen Wishworld minutes. She didn't see how the mission was even possible anymore.

Clover heard sounds from downstairs: voices raised in greeting, Mrs. Marshall saying, "Hello, dear." Ruby's dad must be home.

"Ugh," said Ruby as her phone vibrated with a text. "My mom's still not leaving me alone." She turned the screen so Clover could see the message: DAD AGREES. YOU'RE GROUNDED. AND DON'T LEAVE YOUR ROOM UNTIL IT'S CLEAN! THAT WOULD BE ONE WAY TO PROVE YOU'RE RESPONSIBLE.

Aha! Clover leaped to her feet. Cleaning the room would be a simple solution, an easy way for Ruby to show her maturity.

Clover didn't know whether to laugh or cry. She had the answer. But there wouldn't be enough time to clean up. The room was a wreck.

Clover sighed. It was really too bad. Ruby was so close to achieving her wish. She was a terrific, responsible babysitter. And she seemed to be seriously thinking over Clover's advice about talking to her mom. But Clover was out of time.

She turned, smiling sadly at Ruby. "I need to go home."

"Can't you stay longer?" Ruby pleaded.

"I wish I could!" Clover shook her head, upset. "If only I could make time stand still!" She laughed bitterly. "For everyone but us, of course."

For a moment she visualized time actually standing still, everything coming to a halt: cars and buses stopping; Michaela and Joelle standing in front of the sprinkler, still as statues, the water frozen in place.

"Good-bye, Ruby." Then, before Ruby could say a word, Clover slipped out of the room, leaving the wish ungranted.

CHAPTER
10

In the hall, Clover took a deep breath. Everything seemed oddly quiet. She turned toward the stairs, then gasped. Mrs. Marshall stood at the landing, her finger raised as if she was making a point. She didn't move, didn't blink as Clover slid past. In the kitchen, a man—Ruby's dad—stood unmoving by the table, pouring a glass of juice, the liquid frozen in an orangey arc.

What was going on? Clover peered out the window. A boy was riding a two-wheeled vehicle, flying over a bump. But the wheels weren't turning; the boy wasn't moving; and the vehicle hovered in midair, stuck in place.

A realization dawned on her. Just like she had imagined, time was standing still! And she'd made it happen—that had to be her special talent. Without Lady Stella's reminder, Clover hadn't given her special talent any thought. She hadn't spent a starsec trying to figure it out. But there it was, revealed, like a gift! And she was certainly going to take advantage of it!

But how long will it last? she wondered.

Hurrying back upstairs, Clover couldn't resist waving a hand in front of Mrs. Marshall's face. Clover giggled. No reaction.

Still laughing, she flipped just for fun outside Ruby's bedroom and walked casually inside. "Hey," she said.

"You're back!" Ruby said happily, sitting up in bed, her laptop open.

"Yup, change of plans." It felt good to be spontaneous for once; maybe things didn't always have to follow a routine. "And I'm going to help you clean your room."

"Oh." Ruby slumped back against the pillow. "Great."

"Listen, Ruby." Clover sat next to her, kicking aside two empty tissue boxes. "I've been thinking about your mom and your wish. About how you want her to stop treating you like a baby."

"Let me guess," Ruby said with a smile. "You think cleaning my room will help."

"Absolutely. Let me explain." Clover talked about a

vicious circle of stars—leaving out the "stars" part of the phrase—how Ruby complained about being treated like a baby but actually sometimes acted like one.

"You have to *act* like someone who deserves to be trusted," Clover explained. Hopefully, she didn't sound too much like a parent herself! She lifted a half-eaten chocolate bar off the blanket and added, "Ask permission. Be polite. Cleaning your room would be a good first step to gaining their trust. And then your wish could come true!"

"Maybe later," Ruby said, going back to her laptop. "Let's just—"

"No!" Clover interrupted loudly. It had to be done then, while time was frozen, so she could collect the wish energy and still be able to get back home. "Can you play music? That would help get us moving."

At that, Ruby jumped up, fiddling with her phone. Suddenly, music was pumping through the room. Clover couldn't quite make out the lyrics. She heard the word *baby* a lot and not much else. But the song had a danceable beat, and Ruby was clapping her hands in time with the rhythm.

Together, the girls danced around the room, filling garbage and recycling bags, making the bed, dusting the furniture, and folding clothes. They were just slipping the last books onto the shelf when they heard a knock.

Clover grinned. The spell was broken at just the right time!

Ruby went to open the door, but Clover stopped her. "Remember," she said, "you can't act like a little kid anymore. No whining. No surprises like dyeing your hair without asking. And keep your room neat." She paused as she spied a stray sock under the bed. "At least, neater than it's been," she added.

"Ruby?" said Mrs. Marshall from the other side of the door.

Ruby looked at Clover as she reached for the knob. So would she take Clover's advice or not? Clover still wasn't sure.

The door swung open. "Ruby!" Mrs. Marshall gasped when she saw the room. She flung her arms around her daughter. "Look at this room! I can't believe it! How is this even possible? I just—"

"We're fast workers," Clover interrupted.

Ruby laughed. "It is kind of awesome, isn't it? I forgot how much I actually like my room!"

"And you listened to me," Mrs. Marshall said. "That makes me feel respected. And it shows you're acting responsibly."

Meanwhile, Clover tried to make herself as invisible as possible, leafing through a book while the two talked.

"I know I was tough on you," Ruby's mom added.

"Not as tough as I was on you," Ruby said genuinely.

"I'm proud of you, honey."

"Does that mean you'll stop treating me like a pre-schooler?"

"Ruby," Mrs. Marshall said warningly.

"Okay, no attitude." Ruby smiled. "But really, will you trust me more now?"

"Yes. In fact, Mrs. Howard called earlier. She said you did a great job with Michaela and Joelle. She wants to offer you a regular position, babysitting every week."

"Wow!" said Ruby. "I'll make a ton of money! I can buy all the clothes I like—"

"Within reason," her mom said.

Clover held her breath. What would Ruby say to that?

"Within reason," Ruby agreed. Then she grinned. "And could my hair be within reason, too? How about just one teeny streak?"

Mrs. Marshall turned to Clover. "I do like the way Clover has it: very subtle, so it doesn't always show. Can you do it that way? I can help."

"Yes!" said Ruby. "Deal?" She held out her hand for her mom to shake.

"Deal," said Mrs. Marshall, pulling her in for a hug.

Clover let out her breath and felt a tingle travel down her spine. It was happening! She knew it. The wish energy would be released any starsec.

Just then a burst of colors streamed from Ruby straight into Clover's Wish Pendant.

She had done it! She had beat the Countdown Clock. Now all she had to do was hug Ruby good-bye to erase any memory of their meeting, unfold her shooting star, and ride it all the way home. There was just one question left.

What would she find there?

Epilogue

It was late afternoon when Clover landed back on Starland, right behind the hedge maze. Just a few star feet more and she would have been smack in the middle of the maze. And stars knew how long it would have taken her to find her way out.

Smiling, Clover checked her Star-Zap to see if Lady Cordial had called the Star Darlings together for her Wish Blossom presentation. *I can't believe it*, she thought. *I'm the only one to have completed a mission on my own!*

Sure enough, there was a Star Darlings group holo-text waiting. Clover hurried to the Cosmic Transporter. The transporter moved smoothly; the students seemed fine; and the lights were shining brightly. *Everything seems okay,* she thought, relieved. *Maybe the energy short-age is resolving itself. Wouldn't that be starmazing?*

"Hey, you!" Gemma was rushing around other Starlings to catch up to Clover. "I'm starmendously happy to see you!"

Clover grinned. "I'm happy to see you, too—and to be back."

"You have to tell me all about it," Gemma said excit-edly. "I can't believe we didn't even know you went! But first, let me tell you what happened here when . . ."

Gemma kept up a steady stream of talk as they approached the headmistress's office, and Clover didn't end up telling her one thing about the mission. That was just as well. Why make her nervous? Surely Gemma's mission would go better. By then Lady Cordial would have everything under control.

"And Lady Cordial was in such a tizzy!" Gemma was saying. "Piper told her you'd left for your mission, and all of a sudden, she was rushing around her office like a bloombug during a full moon! I guess she was really wor-ried about you, Clover, because as soon as she realized you'd taken the backpack and were better prepared, she calmed down a bit."

Clover was about to mention that the backpack had been empty, anyway, but they were walking into

Lady Cordial's office. Piper was waiting at the door.

"Welcome back, Clover!" she said. "I was sending you good thoughts from the moment you left the Wishworld Surveillance Deck."

"You were?" Clover exclaimed. "Just as I was leaving, I heard a voice giving advice! It said—"

Clover was cut short as the rest of the Star Darlings engulfed her in a group hug, chattering excitedly.

"Come, come, girls," Lady Cordial said, waving off the Star Darlings as she shuffled over to Clover and awkwardly placed an arm around her shoulders. "Job well done."

As everyone took their seats, Lady Cordial continued. "S-s-s-s-star apologies, Clover. I feel terrible you had to leave on your own. Your mission, while a s-s-s-s-success, was highly irregular. Everything about it, in fact, appears to be a bit off. Your Wish Blossom opened before you returned, and your Power Crystal has already been revealed."

Clover's heart sank with disappointment.

Stop it, Clover! she told herself. The most important thing was a successful mission—and she'd brought back wish energy. Besides, she reminded herself, she'd still get her Power Crystal.

"So will you just give it to me now?" she asked.

Lady Cordial shook her head sadly. "With everything going on, I s-s-s-s-seem to have misplaced it. I will continue s-s-s-s-s-searching, I promise you."

"It's fine, Lady Cordial," Clover said quickly. She didn't want to add one more worry to the poor woman's list. "It's all been so odd, anyway, the Power Crystal can wait. But why was my mission so difficult when Lady Stella hasn't been around to cause trouble?"

Lady Cordial stepped back, a strange look on her face. "What could it be?" she whispered. Suddenly, to Clover's shock, she grabbed a starstick from her bun and reached for the backpack. Then she stabbed the star key chain hanging from its loop.

A heavy black cloud spilled out from the star. It floated above the Star Darlings' heads until, bit by bit, it broke apart and disappeared. An icy cold shiver ran down Clover's spine so forcefully that her teeth chattered.

"Is that negative energy?" Clover asked with a gasp. She'd never actually seen it before, never realized it had a color, shape, and form.

"Negative wish energy, to be exact," said Lady Cordial. "Lady S-s-s-s-stella created those key chains. Again, s-s-s-s-star apologies, everyone. I should have realized those could be a danger."

Lady Cordial was so visibly upset that it looked to

Clover like she might cry. "Really, Lady Cordial," she said, "don't worry . . ."

Clover paused, staring at Lady Cordial's skirt. "Your pocket is glowing," she said. A small but bright purple light was beaming from inside.

"It's got to be Clover's Power Crystal!" Cassie rushed over, the other girls right behind her. Lady Cordial reached into her pocket, and there it was, shining for all to see.

"Oh, my s-s-s-stars," said Lady Cordial, turning the brightest shade of purple Clover had ever seen. "Imagine that! I've just been s-s-s-so distracted I'd forgotten where I'd put it!"

She handed Clover the crystal without another word. The whole thing was a bit anticlimactic, Clover had to admit. But she had her lovely Power Crystal, cone-shaped with magenta and mauve swirls and an exquisitely bright orb dangling from the bottom.

It felt smooth and powerful, and holding it gave Clover a sense of strength.

"S-s-s-s-see, girls? Everything is falling into place. We are well on our way to returning S-s-s-s-starland to its earlier brilliant s-s-s-s-state!"

The girls left Lady Cordial's office together, happily talking about the future. "And there's still Gemma's mission!" said Tessa. "That will make everything even better!"

"I know what we should do to celebrate!" Astra jumped up and down with excitement. "Let's hike up in the Crystal Mountains. The suns will be setting. It will be beautiful!"

Leona glanced worriedly at her sandals. "We'll only go to the foothills," Astra assured her. "We don't want to wear anyone out—especially Clover, since she just got back."

Tessa ran to the Celestial Café to pick up a picnic dinner, and starmins later, they were off. The girls followed the trail, talking and laughing and hugging Clover. *This is even better than a boring old ceremony!* Clover thought. She was having so much fun it took her a few starsecs to realize they'd reached the lookout point.

One by one, the Star Darlings took seats along the soft mossy ledge. Tessa handed out star sandwiches and glimmerchips as everyone gazed at the setting suns. Colors filled the sky like Festival of Illumination fireworks. Clover, filled with a sense of well-being, put one arm around Astra and the other around Piper.

Piper turned to her, a worried expression on her face. "I had a dream just like this. I have a strange feeling something's about to happen."

"Stop it, Piper!" Clover said, laughing. "You heard Lady Cordial."

"Look," Piper said quietly, pointing to the view.

Clover gazed over the city and towns spread below, and suddenly, she saw it, too. The lights were flickering. The Star Darlings' voices trailed off as one by one they noticed it. Then, suddenly, the lights were snuffed out. All was dark.

"Oh, *starf*," said Clover. "Things aren't better. They're way worse."

She had a sudden horrible thought. What if Starland faded so much that Wishlings stopped making wishes at all? What would happen then?

The temperature dropped, and she shivered. She'd keep her frightening thoughts to herself for now.

Sage jumped to her feet. "Everybody! Let's get out of here and go someplace warm. My room!"

The girls hurried down the hill, hugging themselves for warmth, relieved when they reached Sage's room.

Clover sat on Sage's comfortable round bed. The room was homey, decorated in soothing shades of lavender, with a holo-photo album running pictures of her life in Starland City. She saw Sage posing with her younger twin brothers.

"I'm more worried than I was before," Cassie said

with a shake of her head. "I just don't know what to think anymore."

"Well, I'll tell you," Scarlet said heatedly. "Nothing has changed. Lady Stella is evil. And things are getting worse even after Clover brought back all that wish energy."

Suddenly, Astra gasped, pointing at the holo-photos. "Oh, my stars. I just saw the woman who's been plotting with Lady Stella!"

"What are you talking about?" Sage asked. "Show us!" She rewound the pictures with a flick of her wrist.

"Stop!" Astra ordered. "There she is! That's the woman who's been meeting with Lady Stella. They've been working together for stars know how long!"

The holo-photo showed a woman in a purple cloak standing next to a laboratory table.

Sage stared at the picture, shaking her head wordlessly.

"What's wrong?" Cassie cried.

"We've made a big mistake," Sage said dully. "Lady Stella can't possibly be evil. I know that woman really well." She raised her head, and her lavender eyes glittered.

"She's my mother."

Glossary

Afterglow: The Starling afterlife. When Starlings die, it is said that they have "begun their afterglow."

Age of Fulfillment: The age at which a Starling is considered mature enough to begin to study wish granting.

Astromuffin: A delicious baked breakfast treat.

Bad Wish Orbs: Orbs that are the result of bad or selfish wishes made on Wishworld. These grow dark and warped and are quickly sent to the Negative Energy Facility.

Big Dipper Dormitory: Where third- and fourth-year students live.

Bot-Bot: A Starland robot. There are Bot-Bot guards, waiters, deliverers, and guides on Starland.

Bright Day: The date a Starling is born, celebrated each year like a Wishling birthday.

Celestial Café: Starling Academy's outstanding cafeteria.

Chatterburst: An orange flower that turns to face whoever is near to capture attention.

Cloud candy: A fluffy, sticky, sweet treat on a stick, similar to Wishworld cotton candy.

Cosmic Transporter: The moving sidewalk system that transports students through dorms and across the Starling Academy campus.

Countdown Clock: A timing device on a Starling's Star-Zap. It lets them know how much time is left on a Wish Mission, which coincides with when the Wish Orb will fade.

Crystal Mountains: The most beautiful mountains on Starland. They are located across the lake from Starling Academy.

Cycle of Life: A Starling's life span. When Starlings die, they are said to have "completed their Cycle of Life."

Dododay: The second starday of the school week. The days in order are Sweetday, Shineday, Dododay, Yumday, Lunaday, Bopday, Reliquaday, and Babsday. (Starlandians have a three-day weekend every starweek.)

floozel: The Starland equivalent of a Wishworld mile.

flutterfocus: A Starland creature similar to a Wishworld butterfly but with illuminated wings.

frisbeam: A disc-shaped piece of sporting equipment that flies through the air when thrown, like a Wishworld Frisbee.

Galliope: A sparkly Starland creature similar to a Wishworld horse.

Garble greens: A Starland vegetable similar to spinach.

Glion: A gentle Starland creature similar in appearance to a Wishworld lion but with a multicolored glowing mane.

Glitterbees: Blue-and-orange-striped bugs that pollinate Starland flowers and produce a sweet substance called delicata.

Glorange: A glowing orange fruit. Its juice is often enjoyed at breakfast time.

Glowfur: A small furry Starland creature with gossamer wings that eats flowers and glows.

Glowzen: A number equating to a Wishworld dozen.

Good Wish Orbs: Orbs that are the result of positive wishes made on Wishworld. They are planted in Wish-Houses.

Googlehorn: A brass musical instrument that resembles a Wishworld trumpet.

Halo Hall: The building where Starling Academy classes are held.

Holo-text: A message received on a Star-Zap and projected into the air. There are also holo-albums, holo-billboards, holo-books, holo-cards, holo-communications, holo-diaries, holo-flyers, holo-letters, holo-papers, holo-pictures, and holo–place cards. Anything that would be made of paper or contain writing or images on Wishworld is a hologram on Starland.

Hydrong: The Starland equivalent of a Wishworld hundred.

Illumination Library: The impressive library at Starling Academy.

Impossible Wish Orbs: Orbs that are the result of wishes made on Wishworld that are beyond the power of Starlings to grant.

Keytar: A musical instrument that looks like a cross between a guitar and a keyboard.

Lightning Lounge: A place on the Starling Academy campus where students relax and socialize.

Little Dipper Dormitory: Where first- and second-year students live.

Luminous Lake: A serene and lovely lake next to the Starling Academy campus.

Mirror Mantra: A saying specific to each Star Darling that when recited gives her (and her Wisher) reassurance and strength. When a Starling recites her Mirror Mantra while looking in a mirror, she will see her true appearance reflected.

Moonberries: Sweet berries that grow on Starland. They are both Tessa's and Lady Stella's favorite snack.

Moonium: An amount similar to a Wishworld million.

Old Prism: A medium-sized historical city about an hour from Starling Academy.

Ozziefruit: Sweet plum-sized indigo fruit that grows on pink-leaved trees and is usually eaten raw or cooked in pies.

Panthera: Clover's Power Crystal—a cone-shaped jewel with magenta and mauve swirls and a bright purple orb dangling from the bottom.

Plantannas: A curved tubelike fruit encased in a glowing yellow peel, somewhat like a cross between Wishworld bananas and plantains.

Power Crystal: The powerful stone each Star Darling receives once she has granted her first wish.

Purple piphany: Clover's Wish Blossom—the petals of this flower are surrounded by five rings of pale purple light.

Radiant Recreation Center: The building at Starling Academy where students take Physical Energy, health, and fitness classes. The rec center has a large gymnasium for exercising, a running track, areas for games, and a sparkling star-pool.

Shooting stars: Speeding stars that Starlings can latch on to and ride to Wishworld.

Sparkle shower: An energy shower Starlings take every day to get clean and refresh their sparkling glow.

Star ball: An intramural sport that shares similarities with soccer on Wishworld, but star ball players use energy manipulation to control the ball.

Starcar: The primary mode of transportation for most Starlings. These ultrasafe vehicles drive themselves on cushions of wish energy.

Star Caves: The caverns underneath Starling Academy, where the Star Darlings' secret Wish Cavern is located.

Starclone: A conical windstorm that can pick up objects and deposit them elsewhere.

Starf!: A Starling expression of dismay.

Star Kindness Day: A special Starland holiday that celebrates spreading kindness, compliments, and good cheer.

Starland City: The largest city on Starland, also its capital.

Starlings: The glowing beings with sparkly skin who live on Starland.

Star Quad: The center of the Starling Academy campus. The dancing fountain, band shell, and hedge maze are located there.

Star salutations: The Starling way to say "thank you."

Starwire: A cable stretched between two high points that circus performers walk across, like a Wishworld tightrope.

Staryear: The Starland equivalent of a Wishworld year.

Star-Zap: The ultimate smartphone, which Starlings use for all communications. It has myriad features.

Stellation: The point of a star. Halo Hall has five stellations, each housing a different department.

Supernova: A stellar explosion. Also used colloquially, meaning "really angry," as in "She went supernova when she found out the bad news."

Time of Letting Go: One of the four seasons on Starland. It falls between the warmest season and the coldest, similar to fall on Wishworld.

Time of Lumiere: The warmest season on Starland, similar to summer on Wishworld.

Time of New Beginnings: Similar to spring on Wishworld, this is the season that follows the coldest time of year; it's when plants and trees come into bloom.

Time of Shadows: The coldest season of the year on Starland, similar to winter on Wishworld.

Toothlight: A high-tech gadget Starlings use to clean their teeth.

Wish Blossom: The bloom that appears from a Wish Orb after its wish is granted.

Wish energy: The positive energy that is released when a wish is granted. Wish energy powers everything on Starland.

Wisher: The Wishling who has made the wish that is being granted.

Wish-Granters: Starlings whose job is to travel down to Wishworld to help make wishes come true and collect wish energy.

Wish-House: The place where Wish Orbs are planted and cared for until they sparkle. Once the orb's wish is granted, it becomes a Wish Blossom.

Wishlings: The inhabitants of Wishworld.

Wish Mission: The task a Starling undertakes when she travels to Wishworld to help grant a wish.

Wish Orb: The form a wish takes on Wishworld before traveling to Starland. There it will grow and sparkle when it's time to grant the wish.

Wish Pendant: A gadget that absorbs and transports wish energy, helps Starlings locate their Wishers, and changes a Starling's appearance. Each Wish Pendant holds a different special power for its Star Darling.

Wishworld: The planet Starland relies on for wish energy. The beings on Wishworld know it by another name—Earth.

Wishworld Outfit Selector: A program on each Star-Zap that accesses Wishworld fashions for Starlings to wear to blend in on their Wish Missions.

Wishworld Surveillance Deck: A platform located high above the campus where Starling Academy students go to observe Wishlings through high-powered telescopes.

Zing: A traditional Starling breakfast drink. It can be enjoyed hot or iced.

Acknowledgments

It is impossible to list all of our gratitude, but we will try.

Our most precious gift and greatest teacher, Halo; we love you more than there are stars in the sky . . . punashaku. To the rest of our crazy, awesome, unique tribe—thank you for teaching us to go for our dreams. Integrity. Strength. Love. Foundation. Family. Grateful. Mimi Muldoon—from your star doodling to naming our Star Darlings, your artistry, unconditional love, and inspiration is infinite. Didi Muldoon—your belief and support in us is only matched by your fierce protection and massive-hearted guidance. Gail. Queen G. Your business sense and witchy wisdom are legendary. Frank—you are missed and we know you are watching over us all. Along with Tutu, Nana, and Deda, who are always present, gently guiding us in spirit. To our colorful, totally genius, and bananas siblings—Patrick, Moon, Diva, and Dweezil—there is more creativity and humor in those four names than most people experience in a lifetime. Blessed. To our magical nieces—Mathilda, Zola, Ceylon, and Mia—the Star Darlings adore you and so do we. Our witchy cuzzie fairy godmothers—Ane and Gina. Our fairy fashion godfather, Paris. Our sweet Panay. Teeta and Freddy—we love you all so much. And our four-legged fur babies—Sandwich, Luna, Figgy, and Pinky Star.

The incredible Barry Waldo, our SD partner. Sent to us from above in perfect timing. Your expertise and friendship are beyond words. We love you and Gary to the moon and back. Long live the manifestation room!

Catherine Daly—the stars shined brightly upon us the day we aligned with you. Your talent and inspiration are otherworldly; our appreciation cannot be expressed in words. Many heartfelt hugs for you and the adorable Oonagh.

To our beloved Disney family. Thank you for believing in us. Wendy Lefkon, our master guide and friend through this entire journey. Stephanie Lurie, for being the first to believe in Star Darlings. Suzanne Murphy, who helped every step of the way. Jeanne Mosure, we fell in love with you the first time we met, and Star Darlings wouldn't be what it is without you. Andrew Sugerman, thank you so much for all your support.

Our team . . . Devon (pony pants) and our Monsterfoot crew—so grateful. Richard Scheltinga—our angel and protector. Chris Abramson—thank you! Special appreciation to Richard Thompson, John LaViolette, Swanna, Mario, and Sam.

To our friends old and new—we are so grateful to be on this rad journey that is life with you all. Fay. Jorja. Chandra. Sananda. Sandy. Kathryn. Louise. What wisdom and strength you share. Ruth, Mike, and the rest of our magical Wagon Wheel bunch—how lucky we are. How inspiring you are. We love you.

Last—we have immeasurable gratitude for every person we've met along our journey, for all the good and the bad; it is all a gift. From the bottom of our hearts we thank you for touching our lives.

Shana Muldoon Zappa is a jewelry designer and writer who was born and raised in Los Angeles. She has an endless imagination and a passion to inspire positivity through her many artistic endeavors. She and her husband, Ahmet Zappa, collaborated on Star Darlings especially for their magical little girl and biggest inspiration, Halo Violetta Zappa.

Ahmet Zappa is the *New York Times* best-selling author of *Because I'm Your Dad* and *The Monstrous Memoirs of a Mighty McFearless*. He writes and produces films and television shows and loves pancakes, unicorns, and making funny faces for Halo and Shana.

Gemma and the Worst Wish Ever

Gemma frowned and narrowed her eyes at her Star-Zap's screen, trying to use the sheer force of her will to make it chime and flash with an incoming message from Lady Stella. When she looked up, the rest of the Star Darlings were looking back at her quite oddly. *Must be nerves*, she thought. Everyone was on edge, waiting for the headmistress's response.

"Any starmin now," Gemma said encouragingly. "Any starmin now I'm sure we'll be hearing from Lady Stella. Actually, she's probably holo-typing like mad right now, writing to let us know that there are no hard feelings! She's an intelligent, reasonable woman. She's got to understand that all the evidence was clearly point-ing at her. We actually had no choice but to believe she was the culprit." She caught her breath and thought for a moment. "Although, come to think of it, she actually could be quite angry with us. We *did* falsely accuse her of sabotaging us. And at the very least, she's most likely disappointed in us for not trusting her. I mean, she was our headmistress. What were we thinking! But . . . it's quite likely she's simply relieved that we came around to believing in her. I mean, she just disappeared in a puff of smoke as soon as we started talking. What were we supposed to think? She could have explained, convinced us we were wrong. Instead, she vanished! Well, hopefully she's forgiven us and she'll have an idea about how we're supposed to save Starland that she'll share with us. We certainly haven't been able to figure that out on our own! Oh, my stars, I just hope she's not mad at us for doubting her. The truth of the matter is that we really should have—"

"Gemma!" said Adora in a warning tone.

"Yes?" said Gemma, turning toward the tall, slender girl with the sky-blue aura. Gemma had just been getting warmed up and, frankly, resented the interruption.

Adora's response was to put both index fingers to her temples in the classic Starlandian "zip it" signal. Gemma gave the girl a "What in the stars do you mean?" look. Cool, calm Adora might not need Gemma's words of comfort, but clearly the rest of the group did. Although Piper had just begun to meditate, her long green ponytail draped over her shoulder like a lovely ripple of seawater, her eyes kept popping open. Cassie was taking off her immaculate star-shaped glasses and unnecessarily polishing them on the hem of her gauzy silver sweater for what was at least the fourth time. And upside-down Astra, who could effortlessly walk on her hands through an obstacle course with her eyes closed, had just clumsily bumped into Clover. That caused the girl to drop the three ozziefruits she was juggling to the floor. Tessa, Gemma's big sister, absentmindedly picked one up and took a big bite. "Tessa!" snapped the usually starmazingly patient Clover. Tessa turned to her, her lips darkened with the indigo juice. "Sorry," she said. "I get even hungrier when I'm worried." Clover looked like she was going to say something else, then picked up a substitute glorange from a bowl on the table. But instead of returning to juggling, she sighed and sat down next to Leona, who was fiddling around with her portable microphone.

Clearly her friends needed a pep talk. With a quick glance at Adora, Gemma opened her mouth, about to launch into some pleasant chatter, sure to calm the group. Yes, Gemma knew she was a talker. A chirpy, cheerful chatterbox. Gaps in conversation seemed empty and were uncomfortable for her. Why stand there in uneasy silence when she could fill it with a joke, an interesting observation, or just some friendly chitchat? She had a lot to say about everything—and anything—under the suns, and she always had the confidence to state what was on her mind. It puzzled her to no end that this ability of hers could occasionally irritate those around her. (She noted that those who did not appreciate her ability generally either had a lot less to say or were lacking the confidence to speak up.) But she knew that her talkativeness could be quite handy for her fellow classmates. She had come to Cassie's aid more than once when the quiet girl had been called on unexpectedly in class, blushing a stunning shade of silver as she tried to gather her thoughts. And during those awkward lulls in conversation among acquaintances, when everyone was standing around, looking at their feet, searching for something to talk about, Gemma always knew exactly what to say. If she didn't, she made something up.

"You have the gift of gab, my starshine," her grandmother used to tell her. That was exactly how Gemma saw it, as a great gift. And now it was time to bestow that gift on her fellow Star Darlings. With everyone about to go supernova with edginess, she felt in her heart of hearts that it was her job to make them all feel at ease. Plus, she felt like she was going to burst if she didn't say something—about anything—soon. The silence seemed even heavier and more oppressive to her that day.

Gemma felt a slight tremble in her fingers as a message arrived in her Star-Zap's in-box. Her pulse quickened. This was it! As the phone began to chime and flash, there was a collective sharp intake of breath. Gemma squeezed her eyes shut for a split starsec, then opened them and read the words on-screen aloud: "'Holo-message failure: Star recipient not found.'"

The downcast faces of the other Star Darlings mirrored the way she felt. Disappointed. Scared. Guilty.

Gemma's heart sank. "This is terrible," she said. "Clearly Lady Stella has not forgiven us."

A few of the other girls nodded. "She doesn't want to talk to us," said Tessa. "Not that I can blame her."

"Wait a minute," said Astra. "You mean you think she rejected the message? I'm thinking that it means she's unavailable."

Clover nodded in agreement. "I don't think she's blocking us. If she was, it would have read 'Holo-message rejected.'"

There was silence as everyone tried not to look at each other, wondering why anyone had ever seen fit to block a message from lovely Clover. But she wasn't offering an explanation. Perhaps that was a story for another starday.

"Our message probably didn't even go through," said Sage. "Otherwise we'd have gotten a message like this one." She stood, holding out her Star-Zap. An image of her mother, clad in a lavender cape, popped up. "I'm sorry," her mother's holo-self said, "but I am away on a business trip and cannot be reached. Please try again." Even in hologram form she was beautiful, an older and taller version of Sage with the same large violet eyes, pointy chin, and lavender hair.

"You're right," said Vega. "Lady Stella's Star-Zap should have an outgoing message like that one." She looked more closely at Sage. "Is something wrong?"

Sage took a deep breath. "I know I shouldn't be worried," she said, "but I am. My mom has always been available for calls from us, even on her most classified business trips. This just doesn't feel right to me."

Her roommate, Cassie, reached up to put a comforting hand on Sage's shoulder, and Gemma noticed that it seemed to almost instantly calm the girl. Sage thought for a moment and brightened.

"Hey, I have an idea!" she announced. "We should go tell Lady Cordial the good news. She's been such a mess trying to hold this place together. I mean, it took her star ages to figure out how to start conserving energy on campus. And now she's totally fixated on Starshine Day when it's obvious it needs to be postponed so we can spend our time concentrating on coming up with new and better ways to save energy. I'm positive this will be a big relief to her."

"I like that idea," said Gemma, glad for an opportunity to speak up. "I think that will make Lady Cordial feel so much better." Poor Lady Cordial. She simply wasn't headmistress material, and she had been thrust into the role after the disappearance of Lady Stella. She was quite clearly trying her best, but that wasn't cutting the ballum-blossom sauce, as they said on Starland.

"Shall we go now?" asked Sage.

"Sure," said Leona, jumping to her feet. She grabbed Scarlet's hand and pulled her up. Gemma was surprised that the girl didn't reject the help. But those two had been getting along surprisingly well lately.

Sage pulled open the door, and she, Astra, and Leona led the way as the rest of the girls fell into place behind them, Gemma and Piper taking up the rear. They stepped on the Cosmic Transporter, and Gemma half expected it to start moving them along, as it usually did. But the power to all nonessential machinery had been cut after students had begun to protest Starling Academy's wasteful wish energy practices during the crisis. Now Bot-Bots were set in sleep mode unless absolutely necessary, food choices were limited in the Celestial Café (much to Tessa's chagrin), and doors were opened manually, to name but a few changes.

CONSERVE WISH ENERGY: LEVITATE OBJECTS ONLY WHEN ABSOLUTELY NECESSARY, a flickering holo-sign read. Another proclaimed SPARKLE SHOWER WITH A FRIEND and showed two smiling Starlings showering in bathing suits. That one made Gemma smile, as it was intended to. A little Starlandian humor in the face of an overwhelming situation.

Gemma turned to Piper. "This is good," she said. "I bet Lady Cordial can help us find Lady Stella now that we know she can be trusted. They've been working closely for a while now. She could have an idea of where she might be."

"Mmmmm-hmmm," replied Piper distractedly. In the bright sunlight, her dimmed glow was more apparent to Gemma. She didn't even want to see her own reflection. Sparkle shower rationing made everyone less vibrant. It was disheartening.

Silence fell over the excitedly chattering girls as they pushed open the heavy doors to Halo Hall. The star-marble corridors, usually crowded and bustling, were empty and quiet on this Babsday. Gemma even missed the roaming Bot-Bot guards, which she realized gave her a sense of security. The girls' footfalls echoed ominously in the empty hallways, which suddenly seemed full of looming shadows.

"This is weird," Gemma whispered to Piper, who didn't acknowledge that she had been spoken to.

Apparently, the rest of the group felt the same. Wordlessly, they walked to Lady Stella's—make that Lady Cordial's—no, actually, make that Lady Stella's office. Leona raised her hand to knock, but Sage boldly slid the door open and stepped inside.

The rest of the girls filed in behind her. Gemma was right behind Piper. But Piper held back for a minute. She turned and grabbed Gemma's arm. "Should we be doing this?" she asked. Her eyes seemed clouded and her brow was furrowed. "I—I'm just not sure about this." She bit her lip. "Maybe it will just confuse her more. Maybe we should handle this on our own."

Gemma considered that. But the girls were ener-gized and positive for the first time in a while. It felt good to be doing something, taking action. And they were already there, for stars' sake. She shrugged. "It probably can't hurt," she said.

"Okay," said Piper, though she still looked a bit doubtful. She faced forward and glided through the doorway. And with a deep breath, Gemma stepped inside and pulled the door shut behind her.